PUFFIN BOOKS

SON OF A GUN

Who is looking for revenge on Sheriff Gains?
Why did the prospectors lose their trousers?
What is the significance of Plug Hat Rock?
Where's The Ghost-Who-Rides?
How did Chief Afraid-of-His-Mother get into the picture?
Will Amos save the day?

For the answers to these and other questions PLEASE READ ON.

SON OF A GUN

Janet & Allan Ahlberg

PUFFIN BOOKS

PUFFIN BOOKS

Published by the Penguin Group
27 Wrights Lane, London w8 5tz, England
Viking Penguin Inc., 40 West 23rd Street, New York, New York 10010, USA
Penguin Books Australia Ltd, Ringwood, Victoria, Australia
Penguin Books Canada Ltd, 2801 John Street, Markham, Ontario, Canada l3r 1b4
Penguin Books (NZ) Ltd, 182–190 Wairau Road, Auckland 10, New Zealand

Penguin Books Ltd, Registered Offices: Harmondsworth, Middlesex, England

First published by William Heinemann Ltd 1979
Published in Puffin Books 1989
1 3 5 7 9 10 8 6 4 2

Made and printed in Great Britain by
Richard Clay Ltd, Bungay, Suffolk
Filmset in Baskerville

CONTENTS

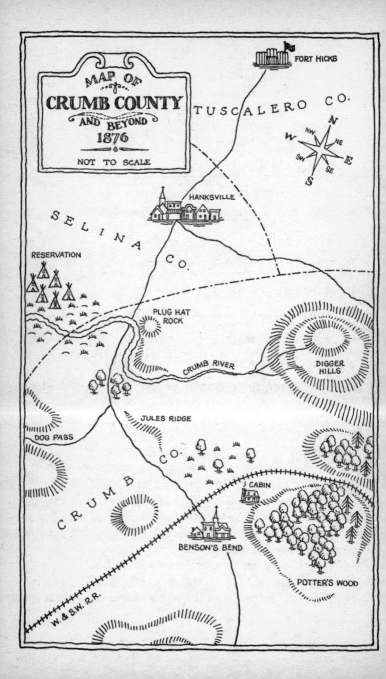

1

BENSON'S BEND

THIS is a story of the Old West. These are the main people in it: Sheriff Osgood Cabel Gains; Mrs Osgood Cabel Gains and baby—this baby hardly has a name yet, though they were beginning to call it Emily; little Amos Gains—this young fellow is eight years old and the hero of the story, you can cheer for him; and the Slocum Boys—they are the villains, mean skunks and a pair of varmints both. Them you can boo.

The other characters are too numerous to mention right now; there must be hundreds of them. Besides, it is poor story-telling, giving the whole game away on the first page, that much I do know.

My name, by the way, is Burl—Joshua Burl. I do not figure in the story but an ancestor of mine does, which is how I first became acquainted with it. I will say, in case it is of interest, that I am seventy years of age and was not even born when these things happened which I now relate.

So here we go. One night the Slocum Boys broke jail in Tuscalero County and went looking for the sheriff who put them there. This was the sheriff of Benson's Bend, Osgood Cabel Gains. We will come to him in a moment.

The Slocum Boys were outlaws: hold-up men, bank sneaks, that kind of thing. But more than that, they were mean. In any game of chance in which they were partaking, poker, say, or chuck-a-luck, they would kick the table over if they were a-losing. They pinched folks' washing off the line, which never would have fit them in a hundred years, just for the meanness of it. They were forever calling some fellow a cissy, especially if they knew he *was* a cissy.

The newspapers of the time were full of their misdeeds, and the court records, too, on the occasions they were apprehended. Take this for instance; it is from the Dodge City *Times*, November 6th, 1873, a point somewhat early in their careers:

'On Sunday last two mean skunks were observed to enter the Southern Presbyterian Church on Front Street and take up a collection. In the space of eight minutes they separated the congregation from: $62.74 in cash money, one ruby ring—value $30, twelve other rings, one silver watch, five cigars, two stage-coach tickets, three pairs of black silk gloves, one jar of pickled fish, one copy of Milward's *Church Music*, and half of one striped stick of candy, which the child's mother said had no business being there anyway. The minister had already made one collection, and they took that too. After which they lit out for parts unknown.'

There you are, that is the type of fellows they were. Incidentally, it is known they committed this crime. They were caught pretty soon after for something else and still had many of the listed items in their possession.

Well, now the Slocum Boys were looking for revenge on Sheriff Gains just because he did his duty and had locked them up. This was more or less a tradition of theirs, getting their own back on sheriffs: on deputies, Pinkerton men and shotgun messengers, too, come to that. They would take trouble over it and could cherish a grudge more successfully than most. All of which was double-bad luck on the sheriff since he never made a habit of catching outlaws.

You see, Sheriff Osgood Cabel Gains, while he was a brave hard-working sheriff, a good husband and a loving parent, was in one respect a plumb misfortunate man. His eyesight was no better than a mole's. In consequence, his aim with a gun was wayward and his sense of direction on a horse most truly defective. You went on a posse with Osgood Cabel Gains, you were liable to wind up all over the place. The truth is, the Slocum Boys' getting caught was more their doing than the Sheriff's. They failed to attend where they were going and rode into a box canyon. Sheriff Gains and his posse happened to come in behind them, and that was that. They were not even looking for them either, but for some other varmints.

News of the Slocum Boys' breaking out reached Benson's Bend early the next morning and not much sooner than the Slocum Boys themselves. Of course, you will appreciate, nobody knew they were heading that way. The news came by telegraph and it read:

FORT HICKS
TUSCALERO CO
25 MAY 1876
SLOCUMS FLOWN. PLUS ONE COPY JUGG'S PLEADINGS AND DEPUTY'S HAT. BELIEVED GONE SOUTH OR EAST. NO HORSES YET. AM IN PURSUIT. YOURN CHAS. H. MOODY. SHERIFF.

The Slocum Boys had been in jail at Fort Hicks awaiting trial for certain crimes committed in Tuscalero County. They had been there six weeks since getting caught by Sheriff Gains. Sheriff Moody had come down to collect them. Now Sheriff Moody was telling Sheriff Gains they were absconded. There was an element of common courtesy here, I guess; plus the hope, no doubt, that Sheriff Gains might go off and catch them again.

Well, Sheriff Gains raised a posse and rode out to do just that. He was a-feared of nobody. Also he had not too much regard for Sheriff Moody, who was reputed to give up whenever the going became in the least bit hard. That was one thing about Sheriff Gains; he never caught anybody, only once in a while, but he never give up.

Before he left, the sheriff kissed Mrs Gains and the baby—kissed the baby on the back of the head, as a matter of fact—and shook hands with Amos. "I expect you to be vigilant, Amos," he said. He knocked over a shotgun by the door, got on his horse and led the posse out through a neighbour's field of corn and up into the hills. Amos and his ma waved them out of sight. Amos waved one of the baby's little hands for it too.

So there you have it. Sheriff Osgood Cabel Gains and most of the able-bodied men in Benson's Bend riding off all over Crumb County and beyond, looking for outlaws. The Slocum Boys a-creeping and a-sneaking on stolen horses up to the Gainses' cabin, a mile or two outside of Benson's Bend, looking for the sheriff.

I will say a word here about the cabin. It was a sizeable affair as cabins go, and was constructed of hewn logs with a clay chimney and shingled roof. The timber came from Potter's Wood. There were three rooms: two up, one down. Each room had a fair-sized window facing south, i.e. to the front of the cabin, with one real titchy window downstairs at the back. There was but one door, though; this also facing south. There was a good cellar and a board floor. There was a porch.

Even for the 1870s this cabin was an old-fashioned place. (Elsewhere in Benson's Bend there were frame houses.) It had been the home of Sheriff Gains on and off for thirty-two years. He was getting near forty at this time; his parents were passed on. In 1853 Sheriff Gains's pa, with young Osgood to help him, had added the stairs and the upper rooms. Sheriff Gains, on the occasion of his moving in with Mrs Gains, had put up the porch. Behind the cabin and down a slope, there was a barn, also the work of Sheriff Gains's pa.

Mrs Gains was feeding the baby with some spoonfuls of mush, and Amos was whittling a stick into the fire when the first shots came crashing through the cabin window. It

was ten-thirty; the posse had been gone about an hour.

Then a mean voice, this was Silas Slocum, commenced to hollering: "You in there, Osgood Gains? Y'big cissy—come on out!"

Then, by and by, a meaner voice, this was Jake Slocum, he *was* meaner: "Come on Gains, it's a fair fight!" He was heard a-laughing. "Just me and my big brother and you!"

Mrs Gains, Amos and the baby were by this time lying on the floor. Mrs Gains had begun pushing an oak table towards the window. She figured to tip it on its end and block the window up. The door, luckily, was shut; it even had the bolt on, a not uncommon practice in that villainous era.

"Amos," said Mrs Gains. She gave the table a heave and over it went. "I do believe those are the Slocum Boys out there. They have come to see your papa and he is not here."

Mrs Gains was noted for a cool and a resourceful woman. Also, she was not about to dismay her own son by outward signs of trepidation.

"Yes, Mama," said Amos. He had gotten hold of the shotgun and was peeking through a crack in the door.

Mrs Gains leaned against the table and surveyed the room. On the far wall a portrait of President Grant had been shot up. Fragments of its jagged glass were hanging out. The medicine chest, too, had been hit and was leaking a steady drip of some patent cure-all or other onto the floor. The piano, though, which of all the furnishings in the room Mrs Gains most prized, was unmarked.

"So this is what we will do," said Mrs Gains. "Amos, come away from the door." More shooting was going on outside, and more shouting, but muffled now; the outlaws had crept in behind a wagon. Mrs Gains fed a spoonful of mush to the baby, who was beginning to fret. "You will go quietly out the back, make haste and fetch your papa." (She aimed for Amos to climb out the titchy window, which with a squeeze he could. It is interesting to speculate that if all this had took place when Amos was nine or even eight and a half, he could not have escaped by this means and we would have had a whole different story.) "I and the baby will remain here."

Amos weighed this up for a minute; he was a thinking boy. He said, "The chickens is in the yard, Mama." Amos had in mind both the safety of these birds and his mama's egg money, which was a source of regular little luxuries in the Gainses' household.

"*Are* in the yard," said Mrs Gains. "They must fend for themselves."

Amos said, "I will follow Papa's trail and shout after him."

"Yes," said Mrs Gains.

Amos put a small wooden buffalo in his pocket—it was right then his most lucky possession—and began crawling towards the window.

"Tell your papa not to delay now," said Mrs Gains. She gave Amos a quick kiss on the cheek, and turned down the collar of his coat, which was sticking up. "He has got visitors, tell him. It is not polite."

"Yes, Mama," said Amos. He kissed his mama in return and snuck out.

Mrs Gains watched him go. She shut the window, fetched down a bag of buckshot off a shelf and picked up the shotgun.

So off went Amos like a jack-rabbit, scooting low in the

13

grass at the back of the cabin down towards the corral where his pony was. Inside the cabin his ma was settling in with the baby for a siege. Up front the Slocum Boys were taking turns to shout all manner of untruthful and insulting observations about Sheriff Osgood Cabel Gains.

Meanwhile, Sheriff Gains himself was up in the Digger Hills with the posse being treated for some nasty cuts and bruises. He had rode into a tree.

2

THE DIGGER HILLS

WHEN Amos had saddled his pony he walked with it till he was out of earshot, rode up a gully and crossed the railroad track, which had come to Benson's Bend about three years previous. It had cut a swathe through Potter's Wood in so doing. Rain clouds were gathering as he set off, spreading huge shadows over the land and hanging low above the hills.

Amos followed the trail, which was easy done, there being upwards of twenty riders in the posse. As you may guess, they were dodging about some. He kept an eye open for signs and portents. An eagle in flight, that was a lucky thing; or a blue trumpet flower—they were usually red. You had to make a wish, if you saw one of them. He took to calling out—Was anybody there? Could they hear him?—that kind of thing. He did some thinking.

15

Amos thought about his ma and the outlaws. He took no stock in outlaws, and figured his ma—than whom there was none braver—was more likely to settle *their* hash. He thought about his pa and the posse, and hoped for a sighting of them soon, or maybe from the peak of the hill. He thought about his dinner—beef and beans, potato pie, a bowl of custard for dessert—that today he was not going to get. Last off, as it became darker on the hills, with the rain clouds lower in the sky, Amos began thinking—and thinking about *not* thinking—about grizzlies.

In school only that week, he had been reading in his *Third McGuffey Reader* about 'The Boy and the Bear'. (By rights Amos should have been in school now, but the teacher was laid up with a fever.) The tale came vividly to Amos's mind. He recollected a picture, too. It showed this little fellow up a tree and the bear after him. Even in the safe haven of the schoolroom with the teacher beside him, that picture had set his spine a-prickling.

Thus it was comforting to Amos that at this time he came upon the company of H. E. Burl and his mules. Mr Burl—this is my ancestor—was sat before the opening of a cave, cooking a turkey on a low fire. When he saw Amos riding up, he raised his hat in greeting.

"Howdy, boy! I'm H. E. Burl, the travellin' drug-store, sewing-machine salesman, barber and occasional minister of the Lord. These here's my mules."

"I am Amos Gains, Mr Burl!" Understandably, taking everything into account, Amos was hollering somewhat. "I am looking for my papa—he is a sheriff!" Amos jumped down from his pony. "Have you seen my papa, Mr Burl?"

"Seen him, *seen* him—I *treated* him not two hours since!" H. E. Burl fanned the fire with his hat. "Yes sir, sold him two boxes of the Burl 'Anti-pain Plaster'; he rid into a tree, y'know. Now there's a thing, there ain't but six trees up here! One bottle of the Burl 'Stomach Bitters' and a pound of snake root. Gid him a haircut too."

"He is looking for the Slocum Boys, Mr Burl!" (You will note that from the larger anxiety Amos had, this accident of his pa's barely registered with him.) "Only—"

"So I heard; mean fellows them. I mixed with them one time. They obliged me to take out one of Silas's teeth—I am a dentist, too, y'know. Then pinched a box of glass eyes I was transportin', and lit out for parts unknown."

"The thing is, Mr Burl, the Slocum Boys are back at the cabin looking for him! My mama is holding them off!"

"By the Eternal—is that so?" H. E. Burl leapt to his feet and spilled a bowl of peas he was shelling. "See here, Amos Gains, if'n I was a younger man (Mr Burl was an older man; grey hair, grey whiskers) and had me a gun—which on account of I'm a minister of the Lord, I don't—I'd *do* somethin' about that!"

The peas, of which neither man nor boy was mindful, went rolling away.

"My mama has a gun, Mr Burl. It is a shotgun. It is a Creedmore shotgun with the end sawed off. I heard her shooting it when I was riding up."

The fire was glowing brightly in the surrounding gloom; hissing, too, with the first spots of rain which were falling. H. E. Burl in an agitated fashion paced back and forth between the turkey and his mules, trying to figure what to do. Amos scuttled along at his coat-tails, hoping to hear something.

Of a sudden, a mighty crack of lightning lit up the sky, followed by a gust of wind and a great roll of thunder. Up there on the exposed side of the hill, it made a noise as loud as Barnum's Drum. As you would expect, the mules and Amos's pony became jittery at this point. They needed soothing and, in the pony's case, a handful of feed before they were calm again.

H. E. Burl said, "Y'will hear the opinion voiced, that th'only safe way to approach a mule is to drop on him from a balloon. Don't y'believe it."

"No, sir."

"Contrariwise, when they say: 'Do not misuse a mule, he will remember you for it', that's good advice."

"Yes, sir." Amos listened a while, his hair plastering to his head, to hear the relevance of these remarks to his ma's predicament. But nothing came.

Thereafter the weather intensified. In no time it was bucketing down, the fire was out, and Amos and H. E. Burl were retreating into the cave. Mr Burl had the presence of mind to bring the turkey. It being more or less cooked, he pronounced a grace and they commenced to eating it.

But there was hardly any light in the cave, and the huge noise of the rain—it was like being in back of a waterfall—made normal conversation impossible. So they felt around for the turkey as best they could, and shouted at each other.

H. E. Burl shouted, "As soon as the weather eases, we'll see about catchin' up with y'pa! After which, we'll see about ridin' back down the Digger Hills, six-guns blazin', utterly to confound and then annihilate (those were his words) the dad-blamed outlaws!"

Amos shouted, "Well, yes, but are we going *now*, Mr Burl? Are we going now?"

I should say Amos never was an uppish boy in normal times. It was the circumstances made the difference.

Elsewhere, on the other side of the hills, Sheriff Gains and the posse were sheltering likewise. Some of the fellows were even managing a little shut-eye. Sheriff Gains, however, was having trouble from twinges in his legs and a cut lip. He had fallen over a grizzly. It was a dead grizzly, which was a consolation, I reckon; just lately shot by a mountain man. Same mountain man, as a matter of fact, that H. E. Burl had traded with for his turkey.

Meanwhile, back at the cabin Mrs Gains was being vigilant with the shotgun. During the morning she had wheeled the piano against the door and, somehow or other, got the haircloth sofa and the club chair on top of it, though it grieved her to do so. She had dragged the bookcase, the highboy and the barrel-framed chair in behind the table which was blocking the window, leaving yet a narrow space on either side for her to shoot from. She had wedged the bread-board in the titchy window and stuffed it up with a rug.

For their part, the Slocum Boys, having been fired on a number of times as they attempted to creep up, were currently getting soaked and blown about by the storm. Silas was eating cold grits; Jake grumbling at the unfairness of it all. "That sheriff's got no business to remain indoors. He oughta be out here strivin' to arrest us. Hell and tarnation—and with his pistols, too, not an unsportin' scattergun!"

In the barn the Gainses' milk cow and chickens had took shelter. The chickens were having a high old time with a bag of seed corn that was by no means their legitimate concern. Of course, an animal will ever eat the choicest grub he can get. The Slocums could not be in the barn; they were obliged to keep watch on the door of the cabin.

The baby, by the way, was fast asleep in a snug little crib tucked out of sight under the stairs. Throughout all the troubles which had occurred and were to follow, this baby, so long as it got the spoonfuls of mush it craved and at the right times, made no complaint. Like H. E. Burl was later to say, this baby was a true Gains! It squawked but once. As you will presently see, this was a most opportune, not to say life-saving, thing to do.

3

THE DIGGER ROAD

COME one o'clock the storm had blown itself out and the rain ceased. Soon Amos and H. E. Burl were making good time up the Digger Hills. Amos's pony was quick and agile on the drenched slope; Burl's mules likewise sure-footed. H. E. Burl had three mules. Two were carrying his merchandise and personal belongings; one was carrying him.

There was no trail to follow now, the storm had took care of that. It was just a matter of scaling the peak and seeing what they could find. Other effects of wind and rain were much in evidence. Clumps of wild tulips and holly-hocks had been laid flat. The aroma of drying grass hung in the air—of drying mule and pony, too. Some of the rocks were beginning to steam. There was a continuous sound of trickling water.

21

At the top of the hill both riders dismounted and looked around. They could see a stretch of prairie running off to the horizon, with a distant squall of rain still blowing about on it. They could see the town of Hanksville to the west, and the old wagon-trail coming down to Hanksville from Fort Hicks and heading on towards the Crumb River. With the aid of a spy-glass which H. E. Burl produced, they could even see the Indian reservation. What they could not see, with or without the spy-glass, was Sheriff Osgood Cabel Gains or his posse.

Amos's spirits slumped. He had been consoling himself for the past hour with the thought of reaching this point, and the promise of what he would find.

H. E. Burl said, "Best to keep movin'; they've got to be around here some place." He caught the look in Amos's eye. "Buck up, young fella! Your ma is noted for a cool and a resourceful woman, she has got a Creedmore shotgun, and that cabin o' yourn is like a little fort! I've knowed it since y'grandpa's time." They commenced on down the other side of the hill. "Yes sir, y'can have my word as a minister of the Lord; I would not take a bet on *six* outlaws gettin' in that place!"

Thereafter, H. E. Burl proceeded to relate the story of two cousins of his, who had in the 1840s held out against a score of Choctaw Indians in a not dissimilar cabin for a whole week: "And all they had was flintlocks!"

This led to further reminiscence on Mr Burl's part. It was a healthy distraction for Amos and a source of melancholy entertainment to himself. He told how as a little child, he collected forty-three spent bullets with his even littler sister after the battle of Tilman's Run. How as a boy, he floated down the western rivers on a flat-boat with his pa. This boat, it was a species of ark. There had been cattle, horses, sheep, fowl, as well as hogs, all over it. He told how in his early manhood, he became a pedlar: "The thrivingest fella anybody ever saw!" He told of the good food, fair prices and reliable weather of those earlier times.

For a further hour Amos and H. E. Burl continued to descend what was a shorter, steeper slope. They ate a quantity of apples, which Mr Burl had in his pack. The mules and pony chomped up the cores. Amos said he would be a Texas Ranger when he was growed, like Mr W. 'Bigfoot' Wallace, who had give a talk at the school. Or he would be a railroad engineer; or a sheriff like his pa. They passed a snake sunning itself on a rock. H. E. Burl sang a hymn.

By and by they saw a cheering thing, which was a spurt of dust way off to the east but coming up fast along the Digger Road. Only it was not the posse, it was the Hanksville stage.

At Amos's urging, he and H. E. Burl hurried down to the road with a plan to intercept the stage and make enquiries after Sheriff Gains. They arrived with time to spare. As the stage approached, voices could be heard; and they were singing:

> "Oh, it's ladies to the centre
> And gents along the row,
> And we'll rally round the cane brake
> And shoot the buffalo!"

The stage was in sight, coming round a bend of the road. H. E. Burl stepped out on his mule and waved his spyglass at the driver for him to stop. With unnatural haste, and to a chorus of whinnying from the horses and shouts from inside the coach—no singing now—the driver complied with the request. He took a metal box from the roof of the coach and threw it onto the road. He raised both hands above his head. He began making a speech.

"There y'are—that's all the gold we got, y'mad devil desperadoes you! Go on, take it! See, I ain't opposin' you in any way. I'm Independence Ike—that don't mean I'm independent, though—I ain't independent! Independence is only the place I come from and where, by Godfrey, if I'd had any sense, I would've stayed. I could've been a shoe salesman."

"Wait a minute, wait a minute!" This was H. E. Burl. "Do we look like desperadoes? You ain't lookin' at us! Look, one man and a boy!"

"Sure, I know, and six more desperate characters sat up in the rocks waitin' to blast my hat off, if'n I make one false move!"

"My name is Amos Gains, Mr Ike. I am not a desperado. My papa is a sheriff!"

"That don't amount to nothin'. My papa was a judge and look at me! All I know is, this life is just one vale of tears and y'can't trust nobody."

It took some time to persuade Independence Ike that his life was not at risk. Even then it was not so much Amos or H. E. Burl who did it, as the passengers. These were five ladies with elegant wardrobes and sweet voices, otherwise known as 'Miss Alice Flimm and the Omaha Gals'. Miss Alice and the Gals were a theatrical troupe, singers and dancers, right then on a tour of certain western states and territories. They were due in Hanksville for one week and would appear twice-nightly at the 'Buck and Wing' saloon.

Anyway, these ladies yelled at Ike out of the windows, having attended—which he would not—to the explanation H. E. Burl was offering.

"Listen to him, driver. He says the boy's mama is in desperate straits!"

"It's a trick," said Ike.

"She's got outlaws after her!"

"We got outlaws after us, is my opinion."

"And there's a little baby, too!"

"Yeah—well, I ain't no baby, fresh from no egg. Nobody's foolin' me!"

At the finish Miss Alice herself climbed out of the coach and sat with Ike. She volunteered to ride shotgun for him. Ike said he did not put his faith in shotgun messengers. They ever did the shooting and the drivers ever got hit. Whereupon Miss Alice tickled him under his arms so that he *had* to put them down, and that was that.

Well, more or less; except then Ike picked up a reference to the Slocum Boys, which set him going again.

"Slocum Boys—did you say 'Slocum Boys'? Now listen here, I've been held up three times by them varmints and every time it's the same! Pinch the gold, pinch the watches and jewelry off the passengers, *kiss* the lady passengers—d'you hear that, Miss Flimm? (The Omaha Gals went, "Oh!") Then, this is the worst, the meanest part, pinch the mail and sit there readin'—*other people's letters*! That ain't only mean, it's nosy."

(I should say, it was Silas read the letters. Jake was not up to reading. He could not read his own name on the 'WANTED' bills put out for him. There again, Silas always read the letters aloud, and Jake listened well enough; so it amounted to the same thing.)

Independence Ike grew more easy in his mind. H. E. Burl sold him a

bottle of the Burl 'Brain Restorer', only fifteen cents, still it
was highway robbery according to Ike. He sat on a wheel
of the coach drinking it. He did not confine himself to the
recommended dose. Amos stood near. He had his questions ready, but was held back by the morose expression
surviving yet on Ike's face.

"You want a swig of this?"

"Thank you, no sir."

Ike corked the bottle and took to studying Amos. "Is
your daddy truly a sheriff?"

"Yes, sir."

"Sheriff Gains?"

"Yes, sir."

"Don't seem likely to me."

A sage hen had come up and was watching them from
the side of the road. Ike said, "Who do y'reckon *you* are
starin' at?"

The sage hen blinked a while, and ran off.

Miss Alice and the Gals were discussing with H. E. Burl
what best to do for Amos in his predicament. Amos came
up and squeezed in among them; he was getting nowhere
with Ike.

The ladies said, "We have not seen Sheriff Gains, nor
his posse."

"We have not seen a soul since the last change of
horses."

"Maybe Hanksville is the place to try!"

H. E. Burl said, "It's a urgent business and it bothers
me I can't raise no gallop on a mule." ("I can raise a
gallop!" Amos said, but was not listened to.) "Yet Hanksville's a good idea. If the posse ain't there nor any news of
it, there'll be the Hanksville sheriff."

The ladies said, "What if the boy was to ride in the coach with us?" ("I can raise a gallop!" Amos said; still not listened to.) "Then you, Mr Burl, could follow on at your own speed with the mules."

H. E. Burl said, "That's a second good idea. It's a cinch bet you ladies have got brains as well as beauty!"

The ladies smiled. "Amen to that," they said.

Amos was reluctant to sit inside the coach. He feared the Gals were out to mother him. It was full of petticoats and feather boas in there. Once previous in his life, he had travelled alone in this way; to his cousins in Topeka. A lady in the coach had sought to mother him then. It was not easy to avoid attentions in a coach, Amos had learned. He would have preferred to sit with Ike, only Miss Alice had the place. His pony was tied on behind to get the breather which it well deserved. Amos knuckled down and got into the coach. The mothering began.

So there you have it. Amos, still looking for his pa, is riding to Hanksville. This was by no means a bad move since at that moment Sheriff Gains was *in* Hanksville; trouble is, he was leaving.

You see, Sheriff Gains and the posse had spent part of the afternoon riding in and out of a box canyon. They had come upon Hanksville unexpected round about three o'clock. Now, after grabbing a quick plate of hash at the Bella Union Hotel, and getting fresh horses from the livery stable, they were off again. The truth is, they could have been off again a lot sooner. However, Sheriff Gains, in removing his saddle from one horse to the other, had caught his arm on the back of Deputy Smout's head. He had sprained his wrist, which needed medical attention. Deputy Smout was knocked unconscious for a time.

Meanwhile, back at the cabin the Slocum Boys were inventing a plan. They had invented two plans already that afternoon, which had got them nowhere. One was to stampede some cattle the Gainses had, straight at the cabin and knock it down. This did not work on account of the cattle were too few and too domesticated. They could be made to walk, so to speak, but running was another matter. Where they had walked was into Mrs Gains's vegetable garden, looking for greens.

The other plan was to push the wagon that was in the yard towards the cabin and creep in behind it. The difficulty here was that it was a heavy wagon and the cabin was up a slope. Conditions were a mite skiddy, too, from the effects of the rain. Before they were even halfway, the Slocum Boys were gasping for breath. Soon the wagon was going backwards and had run them both over. Unfortunately, they escaped serious injury by falling between the wheels. All the same, Jake did graze his ankle, and Silas got stung somewhat about the head by a bunch of nettles. The wagon was tipped up over a cottonwood stump and pretty much smashed in along one side.

Now they were on a third plan. Like the others, it was Silas's idea.

"What we're gonna do is—"

"If I had me a stick of dynamite, we could blow him up!" Jake was fixing a Burl 'Anti-pain Plaster' to his grazed ankle. "Or a nice bomb." The plaster was stolen, of course. "That'd do it."

"What we're gonna do is dig a tunnel." Silas unstrapped a pair of shovels from the back of his saddle.

"Tunnel, yeah! That's good, Silas. We'm good at tunnels."

Which was the truth, since the Slocum Boys most often

used this method when breaking jail. They were probably the long-distance tunnel-digging champions of the entire state. Incidentally, it was to Sheriff Moody's credit that he had took note of this and confined the Slocums to a cell with a thick stone floor. Only then they had dug up through the pineboard ceiling and made an exit there.

"I figure we should dig like this." Silas drew a map in the dirt with his knife. "Along here . . . they've got a cellar down there, y'can bet . . . and then . . ."

"Yeah, that's good, Silas . . . and then—bang, six-guns blazin' right up through the floor! Gimme that shovel."

I will say a word here about this tunnel-digging. The distance to be dug was in the region of fifty feet. (The Slocums could get close, you will appreciate. Their headache was, they could not get *in*.) The tunnel was commenced below a little hump and behind the busted wagon. The slope of the ground meant it didn't need to go down, so much as along a bit and then up. The workings were not visible from the cabin, unless a person climbed onto the roof, that is, which was unlikely. Concerning the time needed to dig such a tunnel, it is hard to judge. The circumstances were not conventional.

The shovels, as you might guess, were stolen. Like the saddles and the horses—and the Burl 'Anti-pain Plasters'—they had been taken without the permission of their owners, from a couple of prospectors on the night of the break-out. The Slocum Boys took the prospectors' boots as well. Not that they needed them you understand, but to slow the fellows down when they were going for help. Took their trousers, too, come to that.

So off went the Slocum Boys digging like gophers. Silas was looking smug on account of it was his plan. Jake even had to stop now and then because he was laughing too much from the pure satisfaction of it all. He had forgot his ankle already. Jake truly got a kick out of digging tunnels. He had been known to say, it was worth being in jail just for the fun of digging himself out. He also got a kick from creeping up on people and frightening them. Thus you can see how it was for Jake: two pleasures in one, and that not counting getting his own back on Sheriff Gains.

The funny thing was, at the time the Slocum Boys were disappearing below ground and putting on a real sweat, they might have walked right up to the cabin unopposed. You see, Mrs Gains had a big fire blazing, in case of anybody coming down the chimney. With its door and windows shut, the cabin had become a mighty stuffy place. (The ventilation from various bullet-holes and broken panes was having scant effect.) In these conditions Mrs Gains had at last dozed off. She was sleeping like a baby, the baby was sleeping like a baby, and a little pan of baby's mush was boiling itself bone-dry on the hob.

4

HANKSVILLE

THE stage reached Hanksville at about five-thirty in the evening. By then Independence Ike had cheered up and begun whistling a perky tune. The ladies, necessarily, were giving thought to their appearance. With the stage still in motion, Miss Alice was trying on a different hat. Ike managed to hold a mirror for her while she did it. Inside the coach the Omaha Gals were busy with powder puffs, rouge blocks and such. Amos had a hard time keeping out of the way.

From being in two states already and a dozen towns, Miss Alice and the Gals well knew what greeting to expect. There would be a crowd, of fellows mostly: cowboys and loafers from the general store; drummers and farmers; gamblers and U.S. cavalrymen on leave; a marshal, maybe; womenfolk and children; a few Indians even. There would be a rough banner stretched across the main street, saying:

WELCOME
TO MISS ALICE AND ALL THE
LOVELY OMAHA GALS!

There would be a whole lot of noise: whistling and shouting, guns going off, dogs barking, boots thumping on the boardwalks, hurdy-gurdies and pianos belting away in the saloons.

Only this time it was different. There *was* a banner across the street, and, allowing for rusty spelling, it did say the expected thing. There were a couple of old-timers getting into a slow fight over who was going to help the pretty women down from the coach. "Come on, come on then!" they were muttering. And, "Lookey out there now, I'm a whistlin' streak when I git goin'!" But that was it; otherwise no crowd, no noise, nothing.

Miss Alice and the Gals got down, unaided, from the coach. Amos followed. Ike declined to budge. The lack of welcome was disappointing to the ladies; confusing, too. They shook their dresses out and looked around. (The old-timers, still squaring up, had herded each other to the far end of the street.)

Amos was fretting, too, as you can imagine. Throughout the ride in the stage he had pinned his hopes on Hanksville: his pa would be there, or this other sheriff Mr Burl had talked of. Now they had arrived and there was nobody; just two old men—and they were no longer to be seen, come to that.

At this point Amos spied a board on which was printed: SHERIFF'S OFFICE. Taking heart, he sped off in that direction. Miss Alice and the Gals, recalled to a knowledge of the boy's predicament, towed on behind.

But the sheriff's office was as deserted as the town, and for the same reason. You see, Sheriff de Grasse—that's his name, his pa was a Frenchman—was off looking for the Slocum Boys. News had come in they were loose and terrorizing folks up north in Tuscalero County. (*How* it had come in, I will explain presently.) Sheriff de Grasse had left town with his posse, all the able-bodied men in Hanksville, more or less the time that Sheriff Gains had come into town with his. They only missed each other by a whisker.

Well, there was a note on the door of the sheriff's office saying: GONE ON A POSSE. Amos, Miss Alice and Co. trooped over to the general store. There was a note in the window saying: GONE ON A POSSE. Amos tried the door even so, but it was locked. One of the Gals said, "How about the saloon?" They went to the saloon—that was not locked—and came upon Independence Ike. He was stood at the bar looking worried again and pouring himself a drink. Propped up at his elbow there was a note saying (you guessed it): GONE ON A POSSE.

The ladies had a close look at themselves in the bar mirror. They studied the work they had done in the coach. They smoothed their eyebrows with a wet finger. Miss Alice removed her hat and put it back at a more pleasing angle. Amos did not look at himself. He could not see above the bar.

Ike poured a round of drinks for the ladies and found a bottle suitable for Amos. The ladies drank and entered into a whispered conversation with Ike. The substance of what they were saying was, "What's to be done?" The substance of Ike's reply was, "Nothin'."

Amos took his bottle and began to prowl impatiently

33

about the saloon. He stuck his head in a back room. A deck of cards was spread out on a green baize cloth, but the room was empty. Amos came to the foot of a wide staircase and shouted up—Was anybody there?—that kind of thing. He got no reply.

By this time Miss Alice and the Gals had finished their drinks and were accepting refills. One of the Gals—the youngest—had begun to weep. The combination of strong liquor and sad circumstances was proving overmuch for her. Miss Alice and the others sympathized, and began to weep themselves.

By and by, they turned their attention to Amos. They petted him, or tried to, for he kept ducking out of the way.

Miss Alice said, "Poor little Amos, what ever can we do for you?"

And the Gals said, "Your papa is not here."

"Nor his posse!"

"The other sheriff neither!"

"Nobody!"

Thereafter the weeping grew louder. The ladies' further comments were broken up and swept away on the flood. "Those terrible mean men . . . sob!"

"And your mama . . . sob!"

"And the little baby, too!"

Ike took no share in the proceedings but averted his gaze. He may have thought he was being got at. When the time was ripe, he poured another round of drinks. He was keeping the tally on a slate.

In the mirror Miss Alice and the Gals could see their nicely rouged-up faces getting ruined by the tears. They wept the more. They bawled. Amos looked shifty, as far as this was possible for a boy with his disposition. The truth is, he had lost faith in the present company's ability to aid him. Glasses started rattling behind the bar.

Amos stepped back a pace or two. He checked that he was unobserved, and snuck into the street.

Amos stood on the boardwalk, thinking somewhat—he was not too happy with the way things were going—and listening out for H. E. Burl and his mules. He untied his pony from the stage and went looking for the livery stable. Amos figured to feed and water the pony, ride back up the trail and find Mr Burl. Maybe he would have an idea what to do next.

5

THE LIVERY STABLE

THE livery stable comprised a corral full of horses, a
smithy, the stables themselves, and an office, in the
open doorway of which a small pig was sitting. As
Amos dismounted and approached, a boot appeared from
inside and kicked the pig into the street. It skidded in a
puddle and ran off squealing. A yellow dog slaking his
thirst at the puddle, got splashed but kept drinking. Then
two old-timers, the same as were earlier having the fight,
came out through the door holding another, larger pig
between them. This pig was likewise thrown into the
street. A few more very little pigs now came scuttling out
and ran after the rest. The old-timers shooed them
off—"You pigs git out o' here!" "This 'ere's a office, it
ain't no pig-pen!"—till they were out of sight. Then they
returned looking quite pally together, as if ganging up on
the pigs had taken precedence over other quarrels they

were having. Then they saw Amos waiting for them.

First old-timer: "You ain't in any ways acquainted with them pigs, is you sonny?"

Amos: "No, sir!" He was hollering again. "My name is Amos Gains!" And following the old-timers back into the office, "My papa is a sheriff! Have you seen—"

Second old-timer: "Beats me where they come from. Minute y'back's turned they git in here ..."

First old-timer: "Yeah, settin' up round the stove like they owned the place. Did you say, 'Gains'?" He had removed a bag of baccy from his vest pocket and was rolling a cigarette. "You any kin o' *Osgood* Gains?"

Amos: "Yes, sir; that's my papa. Have you—"

Second old-timer: "Next pig comes through that door, I will ..."

First old-timer: "He ain't here. His *horse* is here!" The old-timer gave his cigarette a lick. "Y'pa's been and gone, sonny—two hours since." And fumbled in his pockets for a match. "He's lookin' for the Slocum Boys, I reckon. And Sheriff de Grasse—he's lookin' for 'em too."

Amos, of course, lost some steam when he heard this news of his pa. In a way it was worse than no news at all.

Amos: "Sheriff de Grasse—is that the Hanksville sheriff, sir?"

First old-timer: "That's him, such as he is." He lit his cigarette and took a puff. "Sheriff de Grasse! He would not have us in his posse, y'know. Claimed we was too old and slow!"

Second old-timer: "Yeah, yet he took that dude piano-player from the saloon!"

Amos: "So which way did they go, sir? My papa and his posse?"

First old-timer: "Well, I'll tell you." The old-timer drew on his cigarette. "He went north; they all did. Y'see—take a seat, sonny—it was like this ..."

Second old-timer: "Hold on there—let me tell it!"

At this point the old-timers proceeded to narrate, in some detail and with a fair measure of accord, the Hanksville end of the story. It seemed news of the Slocum Boys had been brought to Hanksville early that afternoon by a couple of prospectors in long-johns. (You will recall I told you about them.) These fellows were pretty much worn out with walking, and embarrassed because of not having any trousers, which, like I said, the Slocum Boys had stole. And embarrassed again because of the crowd which was waiting to greet them, and which *did* greet them. The crowd was really waiting for Miss Alice and the Omaha Gals. I do not suppose the prospectors took much consolation from that.

So, next thing Sheriff de Grasse rode out with his posse—the old-timers cussing them as they went—and Sheriff Gains rode in with his. Then Sheriff Gains rode out again, only this time on the trail of Sheriff de Grasse, who he now figured to be on the trail of the Slocum Boys. Only, of course, Sheriff de Grasse was not on the trail of the Slocum Boys—or hardly—and even if he had been, it would not have made much difference to Sheriff Gains. He had commenced to getting lost after his own fashion while yet within the town limits. (Sheriff Chas. H. Moody, I can confirm, had give up long since and gone home. He meant to write a report and claim expenses.)

Well, I believe you will have got the pattern of it now, which—in summary, and in case you haven't—was:

1 *The Slocum Boys break jail.*
2 *They jump a couple of prospectors and rob them.*

3 *They continue to Benson's Bend.*
4 *The prospectors footslog it to Hanksville.*
5 *They arrive in Hanksville.*
6 *Sheriff de Grasse departs.*
7 *Sheriff Gains arrives and departs—all of them heading north and east.*
8 *The Slocums, meanwhile, being south and east.*
9 *Amos arrives.*

Now before Sheriff Gains left, the old-timers did make an effort to join *his* posse. Unfortunately, they picked the wrong fellow to ask: Deputy Smout. His ears were still buzzing from getting knocked unconscious by Sheriff Gains. Since he could not make out what they were asking him, and since he ever was a cautious man, he 'listened' for a while and told them, 'no'.

In these circumstances—rebuffed by both posses, the famed belligerency of their natures set at naught—you may anticipate the old-timers' feelings when finally they got to hear the Bensons's Bend end of the story. They sympathized with the situation Mrs Gains was in: "That ain't no job fer a lady!" And condemned the Slocum Boys: "Mean fellas them. Like their old man, he was mean. He throwed me out of a window one time." They spoke of Sheriff de Grasse in ironic terms, and the piano-player from the saloon likewise. They detected certain opportunities for bold action. They became roused up.

The idea for what they could do hit both old-timers in one go. However, being from long acquaintance accustomed to know each other's mind, they did not say straight up what the idea was. They did not even tell Amos to begin with. He had to work it out for himself.

First old-timer: "Can you shoot a gun, sonny?" He opened a battered trunk and took out various guns, plus other items of military equipment. He laid them on the table.

Amos: "Yes, sir."

A smell of gun grease and musty paper hung in the air. Amos picked up a Barnes boot pistol and began hefting it.

First old-timer: "Y'any good with a sword?" Now he was bringing forth a whole armful of cavalry swords, bayonets, Bowie knives, even a Choctaw tomahawk. "How's it feel?" He was referring to the gun.

Amos nodded that it was O.K. but did not speak. He was non-plussed somewhat to have such a handsome and special fire-arm in his hands. Also it had come to him of a sudden what it was the old-timers were planning.

First old-timer: "Suit you? Good—it's yourn. Y'can have it."

Amos: "Have it? Have it to *keep*, sir?"

First old-timer: "That's it. I've got no use for a boot pistol. I can't hardly get m'feet into a boot!" The old-timer dropped the nub of his cigarette to the floor and trod on it. "What age are y'anyway?"

Amos: "Eight, sir—and two months."

First old-timer: "Eight and two months? That's old enough for a gun. I had my first gun when I was three!"

Second old-timer: "Which ain't no record neither. I had mine when—Hey, lookey here!" The old-timer took from the trunk—in which he also had been rooting—an ancient cavalry topcoat and put it on. It was too big for him. "I must've shrunk some since them 'ere days." He found a Jeff Davis hat with a bullet-hole in it and put that on. It fitted. "I guess I will go see about the horses."

But before the old-timer could reach the door, it was

flung open from the other side and Miss Alice came rushing in. "Oh, honey, there you are!" She called back into the street, "He's in hic–here!" Whereupon the Gals came rushing in, with Ike ambling after. It became a mite crowded in the office.

Miss Alice—she had the hiccups—said, "Amos, y'did give us a hic–fright, disappearing off like—Goodness, what's all this?" Her eye had lighted on the spread of fire-arms and so forth covering the table. "I declare, I never *seen* so many guns!"

The Gals had never seen so many either. They gathered at the table, took up various pieces of weaponry and began scrutinizing them. They were not steady in their movements. Independence Ike edged away.

"I had a friend had one of these."

"What's this sweet little thing—a 'derringer'?"

"Is someone going on a war?"

Here at last the old-timers spelled out plain and flat what it was they had in mind.

Second old-timer: "Yes, ma'am, we'm goin' on a war—me, m'cousin and this 'ere boy." He gave his Jeff Davis hat a pull. "The foe is the Slocum Boys and we aim to shoot 'em up!"

First old-timer: "Y'see ladies, his ma is back in Benson's Bend being molested by these outlaws, which ain't hardly fair."

Amos: "She has got a gun, though. It is a shotgun. It is a Creedmore shotgun with—"

Miss Alice: "And there's a baby, too! Oh yes, we hic–heard about it already!"

Amos: "Our cabin is like a fort, Mr Burl says."

A brief exchange of courtesies—which otherwise had got leap-frogged in the rush—now took place. The old-

timers raised their hats. They said they s'pposed Miss
Alice was Miss Alice, warn't she? And these ladies was the
Omaha Gals. Ike and they were already acquainted. It
was the Red Letter Day of the year, they said. They had
their tickets bought twice-nightly for the whole week.

Miss Alice thanked the old-timers kindly. She took the
offer of a chair, which they competed for the privilege of
providing. She sucked a violet cachou to dispose of her
hiccups.

The second old-timer prepared to leave. "Anyways,
you will excuse me ma'am, ladies. This ain't no time for
jawin'. I've gotta see about the horses." With some reluc-
tance—it took will-power to quit the company of so many
and such pretty celebrities—he departed for the stables.

The first old-timer had a number of cartridge boxes and
was laying out piles of ammunition suitable to the various
guns. The Gals, from watching what he did and copying
him, were pretty soon lending a hand. Amos was in there,
too, eager to load his Barnes boot pistol.

Amos had worked out the old-timers' intentions long
since. The first hint had been on their faces when they got
the idea. The clincher was them asking him if he could
shoot a gun. As I have said, the news concerning his pa
had laid Amos low for a spell. The thought in his mind
was: 'I am further from catching up than when I started!'
Now, it appeared, he was to leave off anyway, and return
with the old-timers instead. This scheme, though it went
against the letter of his ma's instructions, cheered Amos
up. He could see the sense of it. Getting the Barnes boot
pistol cheered him up, too.

Amos loaded his gun and watched with fascination as
the old-timer pushed the guns he was loading one after the
other into his belt. He could not figure how there was room

for so many, or why the belt did not come asunder.

Miss Alice remained yet in her chair and concentrated on not hiccuping. It fretted her that some animal with a snout was peeking at her from behind the stove.

Suddenly, one of the Gals let out a yell. Ike jumped. He had been mooning over at the window.

"Hey, why don't we *all* go?"

Whereupon up spoke the others. "Yeah, I can shoot a gun!"

"Me too. I can't hardly hit nothing, but I can shoot!"

"I can shoot; I can hit a gentleman with a chair, too, if it comes to close quarters."

Well, Amos and the old-timer did not object to the recruits. Miss Alice was on her feet now, and vowing she would go. The old-timer admired their pluck, and could foresee the extra fire-power coming in handy. Also he admired *them* and could not easily resist the chance of their continued company. Amos was appreciative of the present switch in his fortunes. He was glad to be setting off under any circumstances.

Miss Alice and the Gals took fire-arms from the table; a few swords too. They rummaged in the trunk for what else they could find—forage caps, cartridge belts and spotted bandanas being especially popular.

"That trunk's a hundred and three years old," the old-timer said. "It was m'pa's. I've ever kept a deal of useful things in there."

One of the Gals came up with a bundle of letters and a baby's wool hat. Another pulled out a fireman's helmet, badly dented.

The old-timer said, "I wore that helmet at the funeral of President Polk in 1849! Y'would've been entertained there, sonny. They had six bands and a mile o' infantry alone!"

At last they were ready for off. Amos, in truth, was more than ready. He had the door open and was in and out like a dog wanting its walk. Unfortunately, however, Ike was less than ready. They had forgot about him.

Ike said, "I ain't goin'. I ain't goin' in no direction that might take me to the Slocum Boys. It never was my life's ambition to do away with m'self!" He folded his arms in stubborn fashion. "And I ain't allowin' no stage of mine to follow an unauthorized route and get shot full o' holes!" It was the Butterfield Stage Company's coach, you understand; but Ike considered himself the custodian of it, which he was.

So then the Gals cajoled Ike but did no good by it. The old-timer observed how there was times that come upon us like a whirlwind, like a cougar on the full jump, when we was called upon to show our grit. Ike looked aggrieved but made no reply. Then there was a commotion outside, which was mostly Amos yelling, and H. E. Burl appeared.

In a flash Ike was forgot again. There was a scramble to put Mr Burl in the picture. He and the old-timers were already acquainted.

H. E. Burl said, "I would've been here sooner, except I collided with some running pigs on the outskirts o' town." When he was in the picture he said, "I'm comin' too!" He chose a weapon from those remaining on the table. Everybody turned back to Ike.

Ike continued to resist. He warn't going, the coach warn't going; not nohow, under no circumstances. Which is most likely how the matter would have stayed. Ike was backed into a corner by the stove. He was backed into a metaphorical corner, too. A man does not readily shift from such a position. Harassment serves only to drive him further in.

However, Amos, for one, could not exactly tell why the stage was needed. "See, there is a wagon out here. You could use that!"

"So we could!" Miss Alice took up the point, or appeared to. "And Mr Burl could drive it for us, I'm sure."

H. E. Burl doffed his hat to signify he could and would.

Whereupon Miss Alice averred it would not be so comfortable as the stage, then laid her ace. "Ike," she said, "could keep an eye on Mr Burl's merchandise and mules, on account of when we are gone he will be left in sole charge of the town—alone."

Ike stood there looking like somebody had opened a hive of bees on him. He was no fool; he knew the town had people in it. It was just that, with outlaws on the loose and all the able-bodied men off chasing them, the other citizens—womenfolk, more timid fellows—were keeping indoors. Yet while he knew this with his brain, his feelings were unconvinced. He was spooked, that is the truth of it, by the silence and seeming desolation of the place.

Likewise, Ike's brain told him the Slocums were in Benson's Bend and that Hanksville was in consequence the safer town. But everybody with a gun was leaving Hanksville. Ike's feelings led him to suppose the Slocums would show up the minute he was on his own. At the finish, feelings, as they most often do, won out over brains. Ike picked up the Choctaw tomahawk from the table, which was all there was left. He said, "Well, maybe on consideration I *will* go;" and slouched forth.

So there you have it. Amos, having set out some eight hours previous to find his pa, is now on his way home with four other fellows instead, plus five ladies from the entertainment business and enough weapons to attack Fort Hicks.

They made a proud, not to say fearsome, sight as they left town. But, save for the yellow dog laid out and scratching on the steps of the Progressive Pool Hall, nobody had the pleasure of it. The old-timers were in front, with Amos on his pony and H. E. Burl on a borrowed horse bringing up the rear. The stage had a little swallow-tailed flag flying from it, which one of the Gals had found in the trunk. It was bristling like a porcupine with carbines, swords and such, all sticking out of the windows.

Meanwhile, at this time—it was about six-thirty—Sheriff Gains was heading for disaster in a patch of river mist nine miles to the southwest. However, being as he had not exactly come to it yet, we will disregard him for the moment.

Back at Benson's Bend the situation was also critical. The Slocum Boys were deep underground and digging like blazes to get into the cabin. Not being used to proper shovels—they were accustomed to dig with tin mugs and bits of floorboard, you understand—the Boys, Jake especially, were getting carried away. From time to time Silas would pop up for a breath of air, and take a few shots at the cabin. But Jake hardly came up at all. Silas brought out the loose dirt and made pit props from the smashed-up wagon. He found candles in the prospectors' saddlebags.

46

He boiled coffee and warmed a pan of beans. Jake mostly went shovelling on, and singing, after a fashion:

> "Farewell old California
> I'm goin' fer away
> Where gold is found more plenty
> In larger lumps, they say."

Oft-times, too, Jake would shout a comment to Silas, such as, "We have come before some famed judges, hey Silas? An' will again." Or, "If that sheriff knowed what was up, he would be long gone for the rear!"

Mrs Gains was wakeful once more and posted at the window. She was thinking—and thinking about *not* thinking—about Amos's prolonged absence. She was inclined to review the dreadful accidents he might have had. There were grizzlies in the Digger Hills, she recalled, and snakes. There again, there were mean skunks in the yard. Situated as she was, it was a worry Mrs Gains could well have done without.

What the Slocums might be doing behind the wagon, she could not tell. Then one of the chickens—a brave or foolish bird, who is to say?—came strutting up and began kicking the fresh dirt with a will. Silas soon put an end to this. He had his arms full with a bag of dirt, or there would have been one less chicken. As it was, he scared it off with a look. But the chicken's exertions had spread the dirt to where it was now visible from the cabin.

"See, Emily." Mrs Gains had the baby in its crib beside her. "Those bad men are digging a trench." Mrs Gains had three flat-irons and a poker beside her, too. These were for the last stand, if it should ever come. "I do believe they fear we may attack them!"

Mrs Gains, you will observe, was too rational to think of

a tunnel being dug in these circumstances. Sometimes it does profit a man to do the unexpected.

One more thing, should you be wondering: the two prospectors were still in Hanksville. They were in bed in the Bella Union Hotel, resting up from all that walking, and hiding away, I dare say, from all that embarrassment. In the bed with them they had a pair of brand new shovels and other items of mining equipment. They were not aiming to lose them a second time. These tools had been donated by the owner of the general store. They were yet without trousers, though. The tailor that was fixing to make them, he went off on the posse.

6

THE CRUMB RIVER

THE stage with its outriders was getting along well.
The wagon trail was hardly inferior to the Digger
Road. For much of the way, the land was on an easy
slope down towards the Crumb River. As you will
appreciate, Amos was beginning to come full circle: first
north over the hills, then west to Hanksville, now south
and veering east for Benson's Bend.

After an hour the party had the river in view, shining
here and there like a strip of mirror, or covered up snug in
the patches of mist I was telling you about. Ahead was
Plug Hat Rock, a landmark in that region, with Plug Hat
Ford alongside, the river crossing for which they were
bound.

Amos, impatience urging him on, was up front now.
The first old-timer was telling him a variety of things in no
particular order.

"In the Yellow Day of 1810, birds stopped singin' and chickens went to roost like it was night." He was recalling an eclipse. The stillness of the air and greenness of the evening light had maybe brought it to mind. "I had a dog then, name o' Jim Pug. He had a double nose, which they do say is the peculiarity of a Russian breed. He could not smell with ere a one." The old-timer paused. Amos took the opportunity to get in a word—"Are we nearly there now, sir?"—but was not listened to. "That was the slowest dog ... Last time I was here, I was in a wagon goin' th'other way. Them was the days! Yes sir, got kicked by a horse on this very spot, I do recall." He began laughing. "Heh—shoved both its hips out of joint, that's a fact. True as I'm eatin' this 'ere bit o' biscuit and Lubb cheese!"

Amos was eating a bit of biscuit and Lubb cheese, too. The Gals had been handing them out, plus other vittles, from a hamper on the way along. With his mouth full, he was spared from commenting on the old-timer's tall-talk, which of course he did not believe. He did not believe about the eclipse or the Russian dog either, but they were the truth.

The second old-timer had dropped back and was riding with H. E. Burl, who from his point of view must have appeared quite a young, well set-up sort of fellow. At this time H. E. Burl was fifty-four years old; the old-timers were both pushing eighty.

"I knowed them Slocums' pa, y'know," the old-timer said. "He was the meanest shove-and-grunt man y'ever saw. He throwed me out of a window one time."

A shove-and-grunt man, should you not know it, was a wrestler.

"I never met him m'self," said H. E. Burl.

50

"Knowed Sheriff Gains's pa, too. He was a honourable and godly man."

"Yeah," said H. E. Burl. "I used to—"

"Knowed *your* pa, come to that. One of them root doctors, warn't 'e? Say, is that a gopher I can see, or a pig?"

H. E. Burl considered contradicting the old-timer about his pa—he never was a root doctor; then thought better of it. It was not usual for him to be out-talked but the old-timers could ever do it. His light did not shine in their company. H. E. Burl looked to where the old-timer was pointing. "It is a gopher," he said.

Getting the stage across Plug Hat Ford was more difficult than it might have been. Because of the rain, the river was running high; swifter, too, by the look of it. The Gals got out to lighten the coach. They would double up with the riders and come over that way. It might not be elegant, but it was called for.

Ike urged the horses on. Miss Alice urged Ike on; she was still sitting beside him. The horses whinnied as they hit the water. Curtains of spray flew up and glittered in the air. The current surged against the coach. A hat-box lost its moorings, lost its lid and sank. Miss Alice yelled, not for the hat-box, which she could not see, but from the excitement. Then, in no time, it was over. The horses gained the further side and drew to a halt. Miss Alice took a deep breath and glanced round to see the riders come. Ike, for his part, flung down the reins and stuck both hands in the air. There was an enormous man with an enormous gun waiting for them on the bank.

This man had on a flexible felt hat, moccasins, and was otherwise dressed in bearskins. He looked a sight wilder than the original owners of them. Even so, to anyone but Ike he was most obviously a mountain man, and, while holding the gun, was by no means pointing it. You will recall the earlier mention of a mountain man. Well, this is not him, this is another one.

It is the case that mountain men were not common in 1876. It had been all up for them in the 1840s, when beaver hats gave way to silk. However, Crumb County had a couple yet, as you can see.

Anyway, the riders got across and Ike was persuaded to leave off surrendering. A conversation ensued, such as it was. You see, the mountain man was a Frenchman—as a matter of fact, he was a cousin of Sheriff de Grasse's—and did not speak much English. I might add, being off on his own eleven months in the year, he did not speak much *French*. Nonetheless, there was a deal of enthusiasm in the party for inviting him along, if it could be done. As the first old-timer said, "With that fire-arm of his'n, he would likely hit the Slocum Boys from here—both of 'em!" (The mountain man's gun was what they call an English punt gun; some kind of military drain-pipe, if you can picture it.)

First H. E. Burl had a try. He recollected to have 'parley-voused' with other Frenchmen on former occasions. He raised his hat: "Howdy, *monsieur*! *Je suis H. E. Burl, le travellin' er* . . ." And that was it. A frown of concentration came on his face. He did not say more. I am assured that Mr Burl did have the French at an earlier period in his life; only it had become derelict from lack of use.

The first old-timer said he would have a go. "I'll employ

the Indian sign language, which I know from havin' been a scout in the Oregon Territory back in 1843." So he did, moving his hands in the necessary way and with a solemn countenance. Nothing happened. But the mountain man was a youngish fellow. It is probable he did not know the signs. He said a few words, though, which for some reason put the old-timer's back up.

"Don't y'go usin' them four-legged words on me, sonny," he said. "I'm a whistlin' streak when I git goin'!"

Now Amos spoke up. He told what he knew—surmising slow English might do the trick—about his pa, his ma, the Slocum Boys, etc. Whereupon the mountain man, who merely seemed wild on account of his hairy clothes and face, did commence to looking mad.

"Slocum Boys?" he hollered. "*Vous avez dit*, 'Slocum Boys'?" Which being translated means, "Slocum Boys? Did you say, 'Slocum Boys'?" However, since nobody knew that's what it meant, he did not get a reply.

The derivation of this outburst was as follows. Two years previous the mountain man had had his washing pinched by the Slocum Boys. Being as he most rarely ever did any washing, the memory of it had stayed with him. Speaking of washing, this is what he was doing in the locality of Plug Hat Ford. He was taking—had just finished taking—his yearly bath in a pool above the rock. Thus, while his skins and moccasins might still have stunk some, he himself was unusually fragrant. He had used two entire bars of the Peep Brothers' 'Special Almond Cream' pressed soap in the process.

By this time everybody had given up on the mountain man. Besides, they were in no position to hang around. The horses concluded drinking at the river. The Gals gave the hems of their dresses a final wring and climbed into the coach. H. E. Burl pulled on a boot he had been shaking out. The party set off; only to be followed, shortly after and at a steady distance, by the mountain man. He was riding one horse and leading a second, loaded with traps and other gear. He was smiling, sort of, and as far as you could tell under all the whiskers. What is more, one of the Gals, name of Miss Sadie, was peeping out of the stage and waving at him with a little hankie.

Now you may begin to guess what had took place. All the time Amos and the rest were trying to get the mountain man to go along with them, Miss Sadie was giving him the eye, in a lady-like way, you understand. The truth is, they would have had a sight more trouble getting rid of him in the finish. Later on, you might infer, Miss Sadie overdid things somewhat. She ended up marrying the fellow.

On they went, picking up what speed they could; the slope was more against them now. The old-timers and H. E. Burl were up front, with Amos nipping in and out among them. He was being a mite persistent with that same question of his: "Are we nearly there now, sir? Are we there, Mr Burl?"

To which the replies came back: "Yeah, nearly there—six more mile should do it."

"So quit fussin'."

"That's it—save y'breath to cool y'porridge!"

At this point H. E. Burl dislodged a boiled sweet from his pocket and passed it to Amos.

The second old-timer said, "It ever was the squeaky wheel what got the grease, in my judgement;" and gained one for himself—a sweet, that is.

By and by, Amos was obliged to tidy up his riding, on account of they were passing through a grove of small cottonwoods, whose low and brushy tops overhung the road. Beyond the grove the shadow of the trees stretched a considerable length, appearing to follow the party on its way. Overhead the sky was clear, with just a smudge of rain cloud to the east. It was light yet, being about eight o'clock.

The mountain man was still trailing them thirty yards back. He looked to be trying to comb his beard. In the coach there was much giggling and shoving, with the other Gals teasing Miss Sadie and she accepting it in good part, but blushing immensely. Miss Sadie, by the way, was the baby of the troupe. She was seventeen. I will give the names of the other Gals: they were Miss Kitty, Miss Loretta and Miss June.

Miss Alice was engaging Ike in conversation. He had become more cheerful again. They were getting nearer the Slocums, of course, but now there was this giant man with the gun to back them up.

"I was acquainted with that boy's pa, you know." Miss Alice waved her parasol in Amos's direction. "Yes indeed. He knocked me down in the street one time."

"When was that?"

"It would be ... two years ago; in Dodge City. At first, I thought this was a gentleman trying to attract my attention, you know how it is. But that is not how it was. He just never seen me coming."

"Yeah, I hear his eyesight ain't so good. Wears glasses, don't 'e?"

"Yes, though on that occasion he did not. Next time I met him he did." Miss Alice felt in her bag and presently took out a scrapbook. It had a velvet binding and gilt edges. The words 'Albany Album' were in gold letters on the spine.

"I had this mishap with some money, which Sheriff Gains was helpful in recovering. It was in the newspapers." She offered to let Ike see the cutting, which was there pasted in the scrapbook along with many more, most of them notices of previous theatrical engagements.

But by this time Ike had ceased attending to her. Temporarily, at least, his interest was transferred elsewhere. To the south, certain puffs of white smoke were rising in a regular fashion from a distant peak.

"By Godfrey," Ike was looking worried again. "Injuns!" He pressed his hat down on his head and swung the stage round in a perilous manner, plumb near tipping it up. Thereafter, with many a fearful glance over his shoulder, he went racing back the way they had come.

I will say a word here about Ike's driving. It was a puzzle to some, how, considering his temperament, Independence Ike should ever have become a stagecoach driver in the first place. But the answer is simple: Ike was good at driving; the neatest man with a team you ever saw. And so he did it because he *could* do it. That is the way of things, I believe. Writing books, selling stomach bitters, driving stagecoaches—a fellow usually gets to do what he can.

The riders had likewise seen the smoke, but paid it less heed. Aside from Amos; he had made a grab for his Barnes boot pistol and was paying it plenty of heed.

"Whoa there, sonny!" the first old-timer said. "That's jest a bonfire, f'sure."

"S'right," the second said. "It don't have the appearance of true Indian smoke to me."

"Me neither," said H. E. Burl. "Anyways, all the

56

Indians hereabouts is these days livin' peaceful on the reservation; have been for some years."

Amos attended to this counsel and was, in part, convinced. He put up his gun. Convincing Ike, though, was another matter. There is little doubt that, except for the mountain man's leaping onto the traces of the leading horses and dragging them to a halt, that stage would have bust all records back to Hanksville, and probably Fort Hicks beyond.

However, the mountain man did do what he did. I think he was motivated by the general consternation on the ladies' faces, plus his own wish not to have one lady in particular hustled off like that.

Efforts then were made at reassuring Ike, which had no effect, and threatening him, which did the trick. What they threatened him was, they would put him off the stage and go on without him.

After this the confused and, as you may suspect, indignant horses were once more turned about. The mountain man dusted himself down and climbed into the saddle. He was not even breathing hard. I guess it took no more for him to stop a team of six, than you or I might need to rein a crawling baby up. Thereto, the signs of an unboastful nature were also evident.

Thus was the journey resumed, with more or less the same formation as before. The road rose and fell across the undulating land. They passed a scrub-oak thicket wherein a man might hide and even a hound not find him. Amos spotted several large hawks, and saw a butterfly, too. At this season he enjoyed to catch butterflies with his coat and keep them in his mama's preserves jars. Amos thought about his mama. He felt his spine a-prickling.

In the coach, with a mind to keep their spirits up, the

Gals were singing sweetly: 'When the Swallows Homeward Fly', 'The Midshipman's Farewell', 'I Sigh For the Hours That Once Were Mine'. They had an extra flag flying now. Miss Loretta had removed her petticoats, still wet from the crossing, and hung them out to dry.

Miss Alice struck up the conversation again. She may have had a plan for soothing Ike with the sound of her voice. She surely knew there was no way he would *listen* to her, being, as he was, so much occupied with his own melancholy thoughts and the business of looking out for Indians. (The smoke was gone; nor were any replies visible on the horizon.)

"As I was saying." Miss Alice ōpened the scrapbook. "There was this item in the newspaper. I'll read it, shall I? Yes." Miss Alice commenced to read. "It is from the Dodge City *Times*: 'On Wednesday a gust of wind removed seven dollars out of the stocking of Miss Alice Flimm'—it says here, 'Slim'; they got that wrong—'as she was walking up Front Street. After a three-hour search, participated in by all the gentry of the town, two dollars were recovered. We had supposed the Kansas wind was of a higher order and did not stoop to such larceny.' They was making a joke there, you see. The wind had got nothing to do with it."

Miss Alice closed her book. "Anyway, it was Sheriff Gains found the two dollars and, being the law-abiding gentleman that he was, handed them over. Come to think of it, it was *eight* dollars I lost..." At that moment an arrow came flying through the air and planted itself in the stage among the luggage. "... They got that wrong as—Goodness!" Two more ˙arrows whirred in and thunked into the side of the stage. They split a panel whereon in blue and gold letters it said: 'Butterfield Stage Co. The Comfortable Ride'.

Considering his previous response to only a hint of danger, Independence Ike took the arrival of the arrows with composure. He did not stop the stage and begin surrendering, or try turning it round; but kept on up the road, muttering somewhat, "I could've been a shoe salesman." He figured, I dare say, there was little else to do. There again, maybe when you have expected the worst all your life and the worst finally comes, it kind of settles your mind. In Ike's case it was official: the worst was finally come. Close by on a ridge stood a line of mounted, armed, and altogether hostile-looking Choctaw Indians. In truth, there were a number of Cherokee, Creek, Seminole and Chickasaw in there besides. They were not charging yet, but they were primed to.

Meanwhile, back at the cabin this was happening.

Silas Slocum was tucked in behind the wagon taking pot-shots at Mrs Gains; she was peeking round a corner of the window taking pot-shots at him; the baby was snoozing with its thumb in its mouth under the stairs; and Jake Slocum, in back of Mrs Gains and unbeknownst, was coming up through the cellar trap with a grimy smile on his face and a stolen six-gun in his hand.

So they had done it, you see—a fifty-foot tunnel in less than six hours! I would not have took bets on it, but there you are.

Ordinarily, there was a rug covering the trap, but Mrs Gains had took it away for blocking off the titchy window. Oft-times, too, the hinges creaked when it was opened. This time they were silent.

Jake advanced into the room. It flummoxed him, not finding the sheriff but just a woman with a shotgun. This was not the way it should be. He had been rehearsing the scene in his head for some time; had a speech all ready. In the finish, he crept in close, grabbed the gun from Mrs Gains's hands and spoke up anyway: "Gotcha!"

But the scene continued to go awry by Jake's reckoning. Mrs Gains was captured right enough, only she never jumped.

7

JULES RIDGE

IN later years the affray at Jules Ridge—that was the name of the place—was often referred to as a separate matter, unconnected with the Slocum Boys or the siege at Benson's Bend. But it was not so, since without the Slocum Boys there never would have been a 'Jules Ridge'. I don't just mean the stage would not have been there; the *Indians* would not have been there. This is not to say these Indians were any more content with having had a country stole off them, than the next Indian. Merely that on this occasion the immediate provocation for their war-like acts was something else.

But I am getting ahead of myself. First, I must tell about the battle. The Indians, you will recall, were in a line along Jules Ridge. They had come up from the further side with all the neatness of a theatrical chorus and all the silence of a spook. No one in the party ever saw them when they were arriving, only when they were there. However, they were not silent now. They had commenced to making all kinds of a racket, with clubs and bows banging on buckskin shields, and much whooping and yelling besides. But yet they never came down off the ridge.

Maybe it was the Indians being stationary like this, encouraged Ike to keep on going at a steady rate, and the riders also. You see, sometimes chases get started from the front, so to speak. Folks—and cats, for that matter—have found themselves pursued for no better reason than that they ran off.

Unfortunately, how things would have come out in this case won't ever be known; for the party had advanced but a short distance, when tragedy struck. The stage hit a run of pot-holes in the road, Miss Kitty's finger squeezed involuntary on the trigger of the Henry rifle she was holding, the gun went off, and the ball flew up the ridge and took away the end of the Choctaw chief's feathered lance, which *he* was holding. Whereupon he gave some kind of signal with what was left of it, and the Indians charged. This chief was Chief Afraid-of-His-Mother; we will return to him in a moment.

So, off they went, stage and riders, 'hell for leather' along the road with upwards of a hundred noisy, mad Indians coming after. Independence Ike, while ever fearing for an arrow in his hat, or worse, stuck to his driving. The Gals with good sense lowered the canvas curtains on the windows of the stage. Miss Alice, a mite less rational, put up her parasol.

Among the outriders, reactions were various. Amos was riding bravely while thinking how his present run of luck had likely come to an end. There again, maybe nothing is ever *all* bad. At least he had the consolation that at this rate they would be in Benson's Bend in no time—if they were going to be there at all. His Barnes boot pistol, by the way, had still to be fired. It proved too much to handle on a galloping pony.

H. E. Burl got off a few shots while yet allowing the words of the psalmist to go through his mind: 'Fret not thyself of evil-doers, for they shall soon be cut down like the grass and wither as the green herb', which was a consolation to *him*.

The mountain man had abandoned his pack-horse and closed-up on the stage. He was keeping in the rear which was a blind-spot for the ladies' somewhat indiscriminate shooting. Miss Loretta, in particular, was acting real lively. She was dodging across from one window to the other. Miss June, confusing this enthusiasm with talent, was loading for her.

The old-timers, for their part, were joyful; popping away with the multitude of guns each of them was armed with; racing their horses (Who said they was too slow?) out wide on the flanks, then up ahead, then back, in reckless disregard of Choctaws and Miss Loretta both. The regrets and aggravations of the afternoon were forgot; the wonted pepperiness of their natures about faded away. When either one of them came near the stage or the other riders, he hollered words of hope and uplift.

Thus, to Amos: "Keep y'head down and ride, sonny!"

"Yes, sir."

"Y'doin' fine!"

"Thank you, sir."

"Y'ever favoured goin' faster, anyway!"

And to H. E. Burl: "This is a reg'lar bang-all, ain't it, H.E.?"

"Yeah, I—"

"But we'll lick 'em yet!"

"We will?"

"'One shall chase a thousan' and two put ten thousan' to flight', scripture says."

And to Ike: "Brace up, Ike!"

"Brace up y'self!"

"Y'doin' fine!"

"Doin' fine? I never spoke a rough word to a Indian!"

Now you should understand that all this and much else was happening in an instant, and that furthermore the Indians were not loitering either, by no means. They were come down off the ridge, the line of them bending to a curve like buffalo horns behind the fleeing group. They were set to outflank it, circle it and snuff it out. As they drew nearer, the Indians poured a deadly fire upon the stage and riders. Leastways it should have been deadly. There were fellows in that tribe could hit a button or a bit of stick at forty yards, with gun or bow.

Well, some hits were made, I can record. The first old-timer had the pommel shot off his Hungarian saddle. The second took a charge of buckshot through his baggy cavalry coat, but this was from the stage. The old-timer never had a scratch; the coat was done for. The stage itself

was prickled over with arrows and looking more like a porcupine than ever. Miss Alice received an arrow, too, in her 'Frisco bustle, which from the distractions of the fight she never even noticed.

Otherwise no damage was done at this time. Since this hardly appears likely, I will endeavour to explain. These particular Indians were, many of them, younger fellows. They had missed the famous wars of earlier years and were currently much bored with reservation life. The opportunity for a chase of this kind was rare. So, understandably I suppose, they were making a day of it. In short, they would defer bumping everybody off, though this remained pretty much their intention.

Casualties were low on the Choctaw side also. The chief's lance had had it, and one not too smart Indian had simply fell off his horse. That was about all. Of course, the skill at arms of the shootists they were opposed by was not great. H. E. Burl, as you know, was never a gunman; and the old-timers were rusty. They had not fired a shot in anger for twelve years. The mountain man, though he had a mighty gun, could do nothing with it. Even in ideal conditions, which did not then prevail, it took ten minutes to load. In addition, he and Miss Sadie were much employed during this period in looking out for each other.

Anyway, that is how it was; and scarce four minutes had gone by since the chief first waved his feathered lance. Then tragedy struck again.

The stage, from the speed it was travelling, left the road, hit a patch of deep loose sand and broke its back axle from the sudden strain. The rear wheels splayed out and fell off. By virtue of his professional reflexes, Ike applied the brake even as they were falling away. He got the horses reined in, too, but the coach ploughed on from its own impetus. There was a sound to set your teeth on edge. Miss Alice covered her ears and in so doing dropped her parasol. The coach reared up on a low bank, and juddered, and stopped.

Now the riders—Amos first, the mountain man close second—gathered round to protect the stage. The wave of

Indians arrived, broke upon the wreck and went flying on from *their* own impetus, well ahead of the foe they were pursuing. Whereupon the first old-timer saw his chance. He gave a sign to the second, leapt back on his horse and lit out in the direction of Plug Hat Ford. Whereupon, misfortunately, a dozen maybe, of the livelier Indians saw what he was up to, and lit out after him.

And all of this had took no more than *two* minutes!

The occupants of the stage were shaken but unhurt. Independence Ike had had an extra scare from the tomahawk in his pocket, which he had forgotten. During the severest jolt it dug in him, leading him to suppose he had been hit. Miss Kitty had bitten her own tongue, but not unduly. One of the swords had snapped itself off at the hilt.

The second old-timer helped the Gals down from the coach. He beat the mountain man to the job. Miss Alice beat *him* to the job; she hopped down on her own.

The old-timer said, "Let us look to our defences!" He began heaving trunks and valises from the stage. The Indians, for reasons of their own, were holding off—reorganizing maybe. "See, all is not lost!" The old-timer had it in mind to raise a rampart for the more exposed side of their position. "My cousin'll get help; he's a formidable man!" The old-timer shaded his eyes and gazed to where the tiny figures of Indians and his cousin were galloping off. "Yes sir, there's a man what does not know the *name* o' fear!"

A voice said, "Let him apply to me; I know it." Which of course was Ike.

Ike was calming the horses. They were blowing hugely and looking round to see what had occurred. The front wheels of the coach were still spinning on the lip of the bank. When the coach had made that scraping noise, the horses must have feared they had a demon after them. The riders' horses were tethered up and blowing likewise.

Amos and H. E. Burl helped with the luggage, of which, opportunely, there was a ludicrous amount. The ramparts grew.

Amos said, "Do we have to wait here to be rescued, Mr Burl?"

"I reckon so, young fella," said H. E. Burl.

The two of them joined forces to drag a heavy box into the line.

Amos said, "Are those the Indians from the reservation, sir?"

H. E. Burl knelt down behind the barrier of luggage to gauge its effectiveness. "That's them," he said.

Amos crouched beside him. "The ones that was living peaceful?"

"The same."

Elsewhere Miss Loretta and Miss June were re-loading certain of the guns. The mountain man had made a start on his. Miss Sadie stood near. She opened the hamper of vittles and offered him some biscuit and Lubb cheese. He, while never partial to cheese and unable to abide a biscuit, ate them up.

The old-timer began allocating positions along the perimeter of the defences. He instructed the ladies in which direction they were to fire. I suppose there was an extra element of self-interest here; he knew well-enough who'd shot his coat. Independence Ike took a hefty swig of his Burl 'Brain Restorer' and passed the bottle on—to Burl himself, as it happened. Then the Indians came back.

They were riding slow and in a bunch. These were not

usual tactics; maybe they were still making a day of it. The old-timer said, "Hold y'fire ladies, gents too. I will give the word!"

Amos was stationed inside the coach. For almost the only time that day he had become oblivious of his ma's predicament. Currently, the thought in his mind was, 'Supposing I got captured and raised up as an Indian boy!' Amos had his Barnes boot pistol in both hands pointing out of the window. His wooden buffalo and spare cartridges were on the seat beside him.

H. E. Burl and a couple of the Gals were also in the coach, with the old-timer on top. The rest of the party were at the ramparts.

H. E. Burl said, "I'm a member of the 'We Help One Another Association'." He was not talking to anyone in particular. "It's for travellin'-men, pedlars and the like." Or even hardly to himself. He moved the canvas curtain with the barrel of his gun. "I've some insurance there—flood and theft."

At this point Amos recollected Mr Burl's spy-glass and suggested using it. "We could get a better look, sir."

"I reckon not." H. E. Burl shook his head. "We can see too much as it is."

After which Miss Loretta in a whisper to Miss June said, "I could just eat me some baked possum, like my mother makes."

The Indians were coming on. Soon it was possible to observe how surpassing smart and dressed up they were: braided hair and elk hats, buffalo robes trimmed with porcupine quills, fringed leggings and coloured eagles' feathers in abundance. And how well-armed they were too: guns, lances, bows and arrows, tomahawks and ceremonial clubs.

The old-timer rapped on the roof of the coach. "I see a Seminole out there. Wow, I see a Chickasaw, too! This must be somethin' big."

Still they came. Now the party was gripped with a shared dryness of the throat and dampness of the hand. They did not flinch, though, and were prepared to be valiant, I dare say, when the requirement was at last upon them. Even Ike stuck to his post. He had no vim about him, but he stuck there. The old-timer, of course, was the exception. He was as full of beans as ever. When the range was right, he spoke up: "Take aim—the time is nigh!"

What happened next you will not guess. It was about as rare as angels' visits in those parts. The side with the most marked advantage, i.e. the Indians, brought out a flag of truce and sued for peace!

It was accomplished in this fashion. The main body of Indians came to a halt, and the chief, plus one other who was carrying the flag, rode up to the stage. The old-timer and H. E. Burl stepped out to meet the chief and say 'how how' to him. Amos wriggled free of Miss June and followed on behind. He noticed the second Indian's feet, which were small and curiously turned in. The chief made a speech.

In his speech, delivered in good English, the chief enquired after the health of each member of the party, and expressed remorse for the condition of the stage.

He said, "I and my tribe apologize for what has been—we realize now—an undeserved and unprovoked attack." (He did not speak, then or later, of the damage to his lance. An instance, I believe, of the true aristocracy of his nature.)

"An extenuating circumstance," said the chief, "is that I and my tribe have likewise suffered in this way, and are pursuing now the persons responsible with a view to chastising them. In the heat of the moment, we confused you with the aforementioned persons. Only later, when passing close at the time of the crash, did we suspect an error was being made. There are no women in the party we seek; no children either." There was no stage, come to that. However, as you will understand presently, these Indians were in a nervous fettle. They could be excused for observing less than otherwise they might. Also, as I have said, there was an appetite among the younger Indians for action of any kind. They would have chased a tree had it got up and run.

I will say a word here about Chief Afraid-of-His-Mother. He was a man in his middle years with polite ways and a high degree of education, which he had gained in most part from the reading of almanacs. He must have had more commercial and astrological knowledge than any man in Selina County. He spoke three languages, not including his own. These were French, Mexican and English; the last being a source of irritation to the old-timer. He had a smattering of Choctaw himself, which it ever pleased him to use.

Concerning his name, a better translation would have been: Chief In-Awe-of-His-Mother, though he was a-feared of her, too, they all were. His mother's name was Big Noise Woman. Even so, regardless that she *did* have a rough tongue, the foundation of her power was religion. Among the Five Civilized Tribes she was that rare occurrence, a female medicine man. She was skilled at the job. In time of war or when an Indian was going hunting, she would supply 'medicine' for him—charms and stuff. Often as not, these did the trick. In addition, for a suitable fee, she would read the future. She had in her possession a little badger's skull that told her things when the conditions were right.

At the end of his speech the chief presented gifts of shell-beads to Amos and the old-timer, and a cigar-cutter to H. E. Burl. (Don't ask me where the cigar-cutter came from; he had it, he gave it and that is the truth.) It was a further source of irritation to the old-timer that the chief addressed most of his words to H. E. Burl and evidently considered him the leader. What he never knew was, these two had been acquainted in earlier years. In his youth H. E. Burl had done some trading and a bit of dentistry among the Civilized Tribes.

These now were the feelings everybody had. Chief Afraid-of-His-Mother was embarrassed because he had nearly gone to war with women and children. The old-timer was disgruntled and disappointed, too, by the abrupt end to the battle. (The younger Indians were put out on this score likewise.) Other members of the party, excluding Amos, were in a state of such relief, they had for the moment quite forgot the original purpose of their journey. Amos alone had got past this to the point of being once more apprehensive in his ma's behalf.

Of a sudden, Amos had the thought that he, too, would make a gift. Maybe then they could resume their journey. Moreover, he had taken a liking to the chief. Amos gave the chief his wooden buffalo. It was either that or the Barnes boot pistol (which was unthinkable), or nothing.

The chief studied Amos and the buffalo before he spoke. "I am obliged to you for this buffalo, little man. It is a lucky buffalo, I observe."

"Yes, sir, it is."

"Since I could use some luck, I will keep it by me." The chief studied the buffalo a while longer. He took a medal from around his neck and handed it to Amos for him to look at. "This medal is not lucky, but is a reminder to me of earlier years." The medal had the head of Lincoln on it.

Thereafter, the chief stared out over the top of Amos's head and began to reminisce. He spoke of his ownership, and his father's ownership, and his father's father's ownership of the Crumb River country, and the various means by which, in the fullness of time, certain American soldiers had come to deprive him of it.

"They said: 'To whom does this land belong?' And I said: 'To whom does this land belong? I believe it belongs to me. If you ask me for a piece of this land, I would not give it. I cannot spare it and I like it very much. All the country on each side of this river belongs to me.' And I said: 'I hope, my brothers, you will listen to me.'"

The chief replaced the medal round his neck. "They did not listen. Later, they presented me with this."

By now the rest of the party had ventured forth. A measure of hand-shaking and fraternization with the Indians was in progress. Two of the Gals traded scent cards and lace handkerchiefs for eagles' feathers. The mountain man and Miss Sadie shook hands with each other. Independence Ike was seeing to the horses again. He was looking almost calm about it. The truth is, though he did not know it himself yet, Ike was a changed man. He had gone, or rather been took against his will, through the fire of his own worst fears and been tempered by it. Miss Alice was negotiating for the return of her parasol. An Indian had picked it up and was playing 'finders-keepers'.

The chief, from appearing to be somewhat glum, had bucked up again. He conversed with H. E. Burl and the old-timer, too, who would not be left out of it. By and by, he, that is to say the chief, made a remark with regard to

Amos which suggested he believed the boy to be some kin
to H. E. Burl. Amos had not been attending overmuch. He
was tugging at Burl's and the old-timer's coats with the
idea of getting them to leave. (A piece of the old-timer's
coat had come away in his hand.) All the same, he heard
the remark and responded: "No, sir, my name is Amos
Gains. My papa is a sheriff."

Then, for no better reason than that he had been saying
it and thinking it all day, Amos continued, "Have you
seen my papa, sir?"

Here we come to a peculiar thing. The chief was going
to say 'no', that is for sure. He had his mouth open to say
it. Instead, he put a hand to his forehead and narrowed his
eyes like he was seeking to recollect a matter of impor-
tance.

"Would your father be a tall man with eye-glasses, and
his arm in a sling?"

Amos said he did not know about the sling.

"Would he perhaps be riding presently in the company
of many men?"

Amos said, yes, this was the posse.

You see, that was the peculiar thing. Thus far the chief
had heard nothing of Sheriff Gains, the posse, the Slocums
or any of that. It was as if he had a share of his ma's
clairvoyancy in him.

Then, Amos said again, "Did you see him, sir?"

And the chief said, "I believe I did."

8

THE RESERVATION

HOW Chief Afraid-of-His-Mother had seen Sheriff Osgood Cabel Gains—which indeed he had—I will explain, though all was not revealed at this time by the chief, who possessed only his own view of the matter. Even allowing for a touch of double sight, this was incomplete.

Here is how it was. The Indians, upwards of two hundred of them, were gathered in the reservation situated on the north bank of the Crumb River, eight miles downstream from Plug Hat Rock. The time was six-thirty in the evening. A ceremony was going on, presided over by Big Noise Woman. This ceremony had been going on, off and on, for three days. This was the last lap. Fraternal delegates from the other Civilized Tribes were present paying their respects. Everybody, from the littlest baby to the oldest chief, was on his best behaviour and dressed up in his finest go-to-meeting clothes.

The ceremony was the sacred rain ceremony, part of an all-round propitiation of the Earth which the Choctaws regularly went in for at this time of year. You see, there was this 'Wise One Above' and he had a great bird, 'Thunder', that commanded the summer rains . . . I do not understand it all exactly. Anyway, you had to do certain things, and there was a certain routine for doing them. If a mistake was made, you had to start all over. Sometimes the sacred rain ceremony took weeks.

This year the proceedings had gone smoothly. The chief's uncle had had an auspicious dream. Other signs and portents had occurred on cue. Now they were come to the climax. Well, the *rain* was the climax; this was a kind of 'thank you' for it, but necessary too. You never said 'thank you', chances were you never got any more. Maybe I have not made it plain: the Indians, Big Noise Woman in particular, considered they had *caused* that storm round about lunch time, which Amos and H. E. Burl had got caught in on the Digger Hills. At least that is how they figured it, and when you come to think, who of us knows different?

All was ready. The sacred rattles and the ceremonial drumsticks were poised. Chief Afraid-of-His-Mother plus the visiting chiefs were sat together in a place of honour. The crowd was straight-faced and still; even the babies were struck dumb, even the dogs. Big Noise Woman was elevated on a dais, her arms out wide waiting to give the signal.

Then, unexpected, a patch of mist rolled up from the river. There was an outbreak of fidgeting among the infant Indians, and muffled coughs from the grown-ups. Then, more unexpected, a party of riders came blundering in, right through the middle of everything, trod in a couple of the ceremonial drums, bumped a teepee over and went blundering out. Well, you have guessed it; it was Sheriff Osgood Cabel Gains.

In one respect Sheriff Gains and the posse were extra misfortunate. If they had come five minutes sooner, there would have been no mist to obscure the location of the camp. If they had come five minutes later, there would have been one dickens of a noise to warn them they were trespassing. But there it is; they were on time to meet their fate, which is all you can say.

It took a while for the Indians to recover from the shock of this intrusion—they were accustomed to peace, likewise—and from the shame of it. As the chief said, "Those riders never even took their hats off!" Subsequently, it became known that Deputy Smout had made an effort to apologize. It was owing to the clatter of hoofs and crunch of drums he was not heard.

It took a while longer for the Indians to decide what to do—finish the ceremony or finish off the desecrators of it. Big Noise Woman hollered, "We are back to square one whatever!" and flopped down moodily on her dais. Thereafter, the chief took command. Soon they were off, about a hundred of them, all the able-bodied men and boys above the age of twelve, fraternal delegates included.

In the camp the dogs were doing some belated barking. The younger children gazed with wonderment on Big Noise Woman. They were puzzling their little brains about how ever she had worked that last trick.

The circumstances whereby Sheriff Gains and the posse made their escape are not exactly known. However, one patch of mist had got them into their troubles and others, like as not, contributed to getting them out. In addition, the Indians made the error of trying to forecast which way the posse were heading. Whereupon they would take short-cuts and set an ambush for them. It was a favoured Choctaw ploy. But, of course, Sheriff Gains's routes were never that predictable. The consequence was, they kept missing him. In later years, the Indians were to speak most highly of the sheriff's skill on this occasion. He became something of a legend among them, and was given the name, 'Ghost-Who-Rides'.

So the upshot was, Sheriff Gains and the posse simply fell off the earth, as far as the Indians were concerned. You will appreciate now why they were jittery. Furthermore, I believe you will have got the pattern of it, too; which again, in case you haven't, was:

1 *The Slocum Boys break jail.*
2 *Sheriff Gains, in pursuing the Slocum Boys, inadvertently 'attacks' the Indian reservation.*
3 *Amos and his party, in haste to rescue Mrs Gains, from the Slocum Boys, reach Jules Ridge.*
4 *Chief Afraid-of-His-Mother and his party, in haste to capture Sheriff Gains, reach Jules Ridge also.*
5 *The Indians inadvertently attack the stage.*

Incidentally, the smoke signal, it was confirmed, had had nothing to do with it. It was not Indian, neither was it a signal. The chief said it was gibberish. In his opinion some boys were up there fooling around.

Well, the chief's account of all these happenings was

dramatic to a degree. Amos was much startled and could not forbear butting in. All of a sudden he had *two* parents to fret over. When the chief had finished, H. E. Burl and Miss Alice spoke up in Sheriff Gains's defence. Amos, too, when he had recovered his wits, put in a word.

They told how he was really not a wrong-doer, but a courteous and honourable man; not a hooligan, but a vigilante. They told of the posse and the reasons for it. The chief remarked that the name Slocum was not unfamiliar to him. They told of Mrs Gains's predicament; how they were riding to Benson's Bend for to deliver her, and the baby, too, from a cruel siege.

These words had an effect on the chief, you could tell. They aroused his sympathy. Their effect on the old-timer, though, was greater. He had been musing and chuckling to himself at the thought of a hundred Indians out there, roaming plain and hill. He vowed it was like the old days. But mention of Mrs Gains and the Slocum Boys dispelled this reverie and put an added furrow in his much-wrinkled brow.

"Hey, I plumb forgot; there's prospects of a battle yet! What're we waitin' for?"

Which was only the message Amos had been tugging his coat with all that time.

Thus was the action once more hotted up. The chief volunteered the assistance of himself and his men—and his boys—in the rescuing of Mrs Gains. He allowed it was uncommon, but would not hear of a refusal. He did not get a refusal.

Amos remounted his pony and made urgent little gallops, first up the trail, then back. In search of reassurance, he questioned everyone he could, even the mountain man, even the Indians.

"Are we truly going, Mr Burl?"

"What time is it, sir?"

"How far is it?"

"Is it going to be dark before we get there, ma'am?"

"Is it going to rain?"

But, as he had come to expect, Amos did not do too well for replies.

The mountain man had set Miss Sadie on his second horse, which had lately trotted in. The hitch in the proceedings, however, was transport for the other ladies. There were spare horses, from the stage; Ike was going to ride one. But, of the ladies, only Miss Loretta claimed any equestrian skill, and besides there were no saddles.

The old-timer and H. E. Burl were yet working on this, when in the distance shots were heard. Everybody froze. Uneasy smiles and worried glances passed between the two sides. 'It is none of our doing, don't look at us', the glances said. Then a dozen or so of Indians were seen to be approaching from the west, pursued by a single rider. He in turn was being followed by a company of the U.S. Cavalry, two baggage wagons, one supply wagon, one ambulance and a howitzer. It was the first old-timer; him they had all forgot!

The second old-timer threw his Jeff Davis hat in the air—"What did I say? What did I say? He's a formidable man!"—and jumped on it when it came down, an action he was subsequently to regret. For the moment the old-timer had the idea his cousin must have gone to Fort Hicks and back for this cavalry, a trip winged Pegasus could not have made.

There followed a fraught interval when it appeared hostilities might be renewed. The returning Indians were being shot at, and resented the failure of their brothers to

79

do anything about it. The old-timer was doing much of the shooting. It proved an awkward business getting him to stop.

Furthermore, the cavalry were nicely limbered up from their gallop and eager for combat. They were younger fellows, too. Fact is, they were recruits, just left the fort that very day for training exercises on the western plain. The orders were for them to practise bivouacking and so forth. They had crossed the river in the late afternoon and gone as far as Dog Pass before they had observed the 'Indian' smoke and turned back to investigate. By and by, the old-timer had come charging up. He was too puffed to speak, but able to point. Anyway, there were the dozen Indians for evidence of what ailed him.

So, like I said, here were the troopers in combative mood, and there was the wrecked stage and, worse still, the pretty women passengers. Surely some of them needed saving, or showing off to at the least.

But it did come right in the finish. The Indians and the old-timer were made acquainted with the new state of affairs. The officer in charge of the cavalry, his name was Captain Wilkie, was introduced all round and likewise put in the picture.

Captain Wilkie said, "I am delighted to meet you all." He was a very gentlemanly fellow. And he said, "Naturally, if there is rescuing to be done, I and my men will assist by every possible means. Won't we, men?"

The troopers proclaimed their willingness with a lusty cheer.

Captain Wilkie continued. "Moreover, I would be most pleased to offer the accommodation of this ambulance—clean yet and unoccupied with sick or wounded—

to the lovely ladies from the stage!" Which offer, of course, was duly accepted, solving, as it did, the transport problems in one go.

As the ladies hurried aboard, they were attended by the mountain man, the old-timers, Captain Wilkie and a considerable crush of troopers. Captain Wilkie assayed a little joke at this point, about 'stage' coach and 'stage' theatre. Unfortunately, only the chief and Amos cottoned on, and neither of them was in the mood to laugh.

But Captain Wilkie was not put down. When everyone was ready—and Amos was near enough *bursting* with being ready—he made a gallant sweep with his hat. "Then let us all be on our way to . . .," and hesitated; ". . . Burton's Bend!" He was a stranger in those parts; a Charleston man.

So that, more or less, is what they did.

9

THE WICHITA &
SOUTH WESTERN (1)

MEANWHILE, back at Benson's Bend the Slocum Boys had got Mrs Gains and the baby up by the railroad track. They were threatening to tie either or both of them to it, if Mrs Gains would not reveal the true whereabouts of her husband. The Slocums could claim to have pioneered this type of villainy. They did not get the idea from the movies, that is for sure.

Mrs Gains was being steadfast in adversity.

Mrs Gains: "I do not know where he is."

Silas: "Y'have said that already; say somethin' else."

Mrs Gains: "Well, wait for his return. Then you will know where he is. Then you will regret it." Mrs Gains was unwilling to give even the time of day to outlaws. Also, as you are aware, she really did not know where Sheriff Gains was. Come to that, neither did he.

Jake: "What about this baby? Maybe he knows." The baby was on the ground beside the track, still in its crib.

Silas: "Yeah, ask him when did he last see his pa." He began a-laughing to himself.

Jake: "Come on baby—talk!" Jake prodded the baby with a grimy finger. What he knew about babies was nil. The baby smiled.

Mrs Gains: "Stop that! He is a she and too young to know anything!"

Jake prodded the baby some more. This time there was a degree of affability in what he did. He was looking to see the baby smile again. It was a consequence of Jake's trade that he seldom had people smiling at him. The baby obliged. Whereupon, Mrs Gains, not reading Jake's motives aright, stepped up, arms tied behind her, and kicked him on his bad ankle.

Jake: "There!" (howling) "Now y'have done it!" (and hopping around) "An' will be sorry for it too!" He sat down and removed his boot and sock to examine the wound. "Hell and tarnation!" His foot was black. Usually it was grey; it was the tunnel-digging had made the difference.

The baby, set off no doubt by Jake's hollering, had begun hollering, too—fit to bust.

Silas: "Now lady, see here. There's a train due in ..." He consulted his watch. Formerly it had belonged to one of the prospectors. "... eight minutes. So, speak up or—"

Silas's remaining words were crowded out, on account of he had a monstrous sandwich in his hand and was biting into it. His hand was the colour of Jake's foot. There you are, those varmints had no saving graces at all.

I will say a word here about what the Slocum Boys were up to. Ordinarily their motto was, 'Take it and run'. (They had another motto which was, 'It is good to be shifty in a new country'. This, Silas had read in a book.) Well, they had took a fair quantity of items from the Gainses' cabin, viz: two frying pans, two pie pans and a cedarwood pail; three hoes and a Yankee axe; sugar, salt, molasses; one Baptist bible tract, 'Examine Your Hopes For Eternity'; a pair of scissors; a tin of Mason's shoe-blacking—*that,* they never would use; four pieces of yarn-dyed striped cloth; a number of eggs, which had straightways broke; two wooden combs; a lead pen-cil—Amos's; a box of 'Long Nine' cigars that Mrs Gains had hidden away for the sheriff's birthday in a week's time; the shotgun and its ammunition; a hip bath; a copy of Parson Weems's *Life of Washington*; Sheriff Gains's Sun-day suit and his best chesterfield coat; a jar of bear's grease; and an amount of various foodstuffs assembled into two sandwiches, the one which Silas was eating, the other which Jake had already ate.

But they had not run; and this for three reasons.

First, they were still hankering for revenge on Sheriff Gains, and hoped that if they stuck around he might show up.

Second, they were much exasperated by Mrs Gains's coolness; her unwillingness to jump. They were both con-siderably crazed from all that gophering below ground and the disappointing outcome of it. However, in their saner moments they must have guessed that Mrs Gains could tell them little of the sheriff's whereabouts. The ironical thing was, if Mrs Gains had wept, fainted or fell down, the Slocum Boys would likely have left her alone; give her a glass of water even. Well, maybe not that.

As it was, the threats were a bluff. The Slocum Boys would scare Mrs Gains if they could, get information from her if she had it, but otherwise harm her not. Mrs Gains more or less knew this. Extra to her other qualities, she was a smart judge of character, too.

The third reason the Slocums had for not running, was that they were going to rob the train. It had been in the back of their minds to do this ever since the break-out. It was the frosting on the cake, as you might say; revenge being the cake.

This was a good locality for train hold-ups. The gradient and curve conspired to produce just that slowing down of the train which the regular hold-up man prefers. The Slocum Boys had robbed trains twice before on this very spot. Its being the sheriff's doorstep only gave them more to crow over. In addition, the Wichita & South Western Railroad Co. offered a nice class of train to steal from.

The train concerned on this occasion was due in eighteen minutes, not eight. Silas had fibbed about this; in part to turn the screw on Mrs Gains, in part from sheer habit. The Slocum Boys knew all about train times. Their boast was: 'Better than the company itself'. Same way and for the same reason they knew all about stagecoach schedules and the opening and closing habits of banks in four counties. It was professional expertise, though in most other respects the brothers 'warn't no more intellectual than a frog', as they say—Jake especially.

The Slocum Boys were set to go to work. Their guns were loaded; their bandanas turned round in readiness to serve as masks. Each of them had a corn sack handy for the loot.

Silas was approving the landscape. "Y'know, Jake, I do admire this spot for a train job better'n any other." From the height they were at, Silas had a clear view where it suited him, and ample cover—a screen of trees, a further rise in the ground—where it suited him too, i.e. that direction from which the train would arrive. The screen of trees was Potter's Wood. The time, according to his watch, was nine-fifteen. Cloud was gathering above the Digger Hills, but light sufficed yet to illuminate the convenience of the scene.

Silas turned his attention to the baby. The noise was worrying to him. It broke his concentration, which thievery as much as any other enterprise requires, and advertised their presence, which he could do without.

Silas: "That baby will quit its racket or suffer the consequences!" What consequences, Silas had not the least idea. You cannot gag a baby, or threaten it either. A circumstance, I guess, which every parent does discover for himself.

Mrs Gains: "No, it is not her fault. Her routine has been upset. Moreover (here Mrs Gains slipped in a fib of her own), she is in need of gripe water."

The baby was not in need of gripe water. There was no gripe water. Mrs Gains was playing for time. What the baby might have been in need of was more entertainment from Jake and his finger. There again, with babies it is hard to tell.

Jake: "Gripe water?" He was replacing his sock and boot. "Did we pinch any o' that, Silas?"

Mrs Gains: "No, you did not. It remains where it ever was: on the shelf beside the medicine chest."

Jake: "Maybe I should take a look, hey Silas?"

Mrs Gains: "It is a square bottle (Mrs Gains made a neat

job of lying, like she did everything else); the 'Mother Winslow' brand.''

Here the baby let out a well-timed bawl of such magnitude that Jake, without further bidding, went slithering down the bank to where the horses were tethered.

Silas: "Don't hang about, Jake; y'got fifteen minutes."

Silas had been proposing to untie Mrs Gains and get at the baby through her. Happily, the accomplished fact of Jake's departure drove the thought from his mind.

So Jake rode out to the cabin, maybe four hundred yards off, to get the non-existent gripe water. When he was well and truly gone, the baby eased up with its crying and subsided into a light snooze. Silas appeared suspicious but could do nothing for it. He was in any case content with the result, how ever it was come by.

Silas gave thought to removing Mrs Gains and the baby off to the shelter of the trees. He still wished for Mrs Gains to believe that he would tie her to the track, but time was running out. A young jack-rabbit sat up in the grass right close to them and sniffed the breeze. Overhead a mighty bird flew by. Silas recited to himself:

> "A eagle on the wing
> It is a lucky thing."

There was a vibration in the rails. An emerging heavy noise concussed the air. Silas frowned. The vibration throbbed up through the soles of his boots. Then he heard a whistle down the line, and the train came.

Silas stepped back. Though utterly flummoxed, he yet

was cunning enough to grab the baby up and apply a look of practised innocence to his face. In consequence, what the engineer saw, and what the passengers saw, too, as they went fairly slowly by, was just a small domestic idyll: Pa (Silas), plus Ma (Mrs Gains with a gun in her back), plus Baby—wakeful again and flapping with its little arms in plain enjoyment of its little lot.

Thus did one baby by some opportune squawking save the Wichita & South Western Railway Co. a heap of trouble. (You see, if Jake had been there, they would have done the job anyway.) Passengers were not robbed, nor mail-bags ransacked; employees not injured, nor ash-trays, fire-extinguishers, trainmen's hats and such feloniously taken away. Dignity did not suffer, nor was any insurance claimed.

And yet who knew it? Of all the travellers on that train, ne'er a one.

When the train had passed, Silas took out his watch, shook it, cussed it and threw it into the trees. That was the trouble, the watch was slow, not the train early. The service thereabouts was most reliable, as Silas from his own experience knew. In defence of this time-piece, which also had played its part in the scheme of things, I will say that in the possession of its rightful owner it always had kept perfect time. Maybe dirt from the diggings had upset the mechanism. On the other hand it was a *miner's* watch.

Soon Jake came haring up, as far as he was able on such a loaded horse; he had the hip bath and the three hoes among his share. Besides, he was eating a sandwich—hastily assembled—of cheese and pumpkin, Lima-beans and green tomato pickle, apple sauce, basswood honey and a bit of doughnut, slices of crocus bulb which he had mistook for onion, and a piece of jigsaw—Amos's— that had got scooped up with the rest. You may suspect Jake's motives now in being quick off the mark to fetch the gripe water.

Silas was staring dejectedly up the line. The baby was back in its crib being crooned to by Mrs Gains.

Jake: "What train was that?"

Silas told him.

Jake: "Hell and tarnation—when's the next?"

Silas did not reply. He was aggrieved at Jake for being missing at the crucial time.

Jake: "I never got that gripey water." He bit into the sandwich. "Warn't there."

Silas bethought himself some cruel remarks he would make. Sensing his brother's mood, Jake broke a piece from the sandwich and handed it over. Silas wavered, ate it—and cheered up.

Silas: "There ain't no other train till mornin'. Five thirty-one: good for mails, bad for passengers. Ha— double-bad if'n we stop 'em!"

Jake: "Is that right—five thirty-one?" He chewed and looked contemplative. "Ain't it the summer schedule yet? What day is it?"

Thereafter the Slocum Boys went into a huddle concerning train times. The discussion was obscure in parts, but amicable enough. Mrs Gains they more or less ignored. She might have walked away, if it were not for the baby, and she herself being tied up.

The Slocum Boys were pondering now what to do for the best. At least that is what Silas was doing; with Jake it was otherwise.

"Y'know, Silas, I oft-times think if men was women,

there wouldn't be no such thing as dancin'." I believe he meant by this that men would not *choose* to dance, if it was up to them. Why he said it, I cannot tell.

Silas's thoughts were fixed on Sheriff Gains—they were going to have to leave this revenge business for a while, he could see that; and the Hanksville bank—pie pans and molasses were all very well, but what they needed now was cash money; and the weather—it was coming up to rain.

The Slocums' brains ticked on. Faint sounds disturbed the silence: the pawing of a horse and creak of leather; the scrape of Mrs Gains's shoe against a rail. A fly buzzed hopefully around the fast departing remnant of Jake's sandwich. It stood more chance of being eaten than eating, if you ask me. From way off there came the whoop of an Indian.

Jake said, "Silas—(chomp)—I snuff danger."

10

THE WICHITA &
SOUTH WESTERN (2)

WHEN the Slocum Boys saw a combined force of
the U.S. cavalry and Choctaw Indians, plus
assorted riders and vehicles, plus a huge
wheeled gun coming towards them, they turned and ran
like the true cowards they were. Maybe they could not
positively swear the force was seeking them; it was not the
usual-looking posse. There again, the Slocums ever did
have guilty consciences. It was in their disposition to run
off. 'The wicked fleeth when no man pursueth', as they
say.

Among the rescuers, Amos and an Indian were first to
spot the little group away up on the track. The Indian,
from being a high-spirited young fellow, had whooped
before he could stop himself. Fact is, he was hardly more

than Amos's age and had no business being there. What caught Amos's eye was the number in the group—that tallied—and the yellow of his ma's dress with the white of her apron.

"It is my mama!" he hollered. "It is my mama!"

Whereupon the cavalcade altered course; they had been heading for the cabin. Once pointed out, the figure of Mrs Gains became visible to even the oldest, rheumiest eye against the background of increasing gloom. Her 'companions' had run off—so they should. Yet Mrs Gains was not waving, which was a puzzle to some.

Up to this point the old-timers had held the lead. They would not give precedence to Choctaw chiefs or cavalry captains either. Now, however, Amos was coming up at a lick. His pony surely was a game one, and he himself seemed not to be wearied in the least. He might have gone round again! (I guess eight is the age to get things done, if you are going to. When doubt is not known and your muscles feel like they will run for ever.)

As Amos went by, the old-timers, wanting confirmation of his earlier hollering, hollered themselves:

"Is that the lady, sonny?"

"Is that y'ma?"

But Amos had the wind in his ears, and never heard them.

Behind Amos and the old-timers came the others—civilians, soldiers, Indians—all pretty much mixed up together. The ambulance and wagons were to the rear; the mountain man to the rear of them, and H. E. Burl to the rear of him. Mr Burl was puffing hard. The unaccustomed galloping and the unaccustomed horse were beginning to tell; also the all-round fatiguing nature of the day. Anyway, he had not gone into the Digger Hills for trade or employment reasons, but for a bit of peace, which was his partiality once in a while.

The mountain man, for his part, had that second horse which slowed him down, and was besides keeping watch on the ambulance, wherein Miss-Sadie rode.

Independence Ike was sitting with the driver of the ambulance. He itched to take the reins himself. They had quit the road some time since and were crossing an open grassy plain. There was a scattering of ditches and small trees. This driver, this sergeant, for such he was, in Ike's opinion had no skill but was the veriest amateur. They might need the ambulance before he was done with them.

Chief Afraid-of-His-Mother and Captain Wilkie were side by side politely acknowledging each other. They were of like stamp, if they did but know it. Neither wished to offend the other by appearing to seek overall command. They were sensitive of the old-timers' feelings, too.

Thus, in the rapidly fading light, and at an ever-quickening pace, the charge proceeded. The blurring forms of riders and vehicles went flying over the plain. The rattle of wheels and harness, the shouts of braves and troopers, the blast of a bugle even—broke on the night air.

And Amos—you can cheer for him—was showing the way!

Meanwhile, Jake was complaining: "I am as bad off as ever I was!" These were not his first words on the subject, which were unsuitable to print, nor yet his second. Earlier, when they had observed the sudden army which was sprung up against them, he had declared, "What's this—cavalry *and* Indians? Where's the fairness in that?"

At this time the Slocum Boys were minded to run in all

directions. Nor did the panic which was upon them subside. They got on their horses and off them again; commenced to lightening the load of goods they had, then quarrelled over what they should discard. "I *need* them hoes, Silas!" They hesitated to split up or stick together; ride north into the hills or seek a refuge in the badlands to the east. They could not agree how ever they had got into this fix. They were irresolute altogether.

Mrs Gains watched the rescuers as they came on along a wide front, and hoped that she was seeing Amos's pinto pony there at the head. Sheriff Gains she judged to be absent, by virtue of the undeviating character of the charge. The Indians were a puzzle to her.

The Slocum Boys paid no heed to Mrs Gains and the baby. It had not occurred to them to take hostages, a form of meanness they had still to employ. Of course, revenge was what they knew about. "We'll get 'em for this—hey, Silas? All of 'em!"

At the finish, Silas got himself enough organized to climb back in the saddle—"I'm goin', Jake!"—and urge his horse into the cover of Potter's Wood.

"Me too, Silas!" But Jake was dithering yet with his booty—"We'll give 'em the slip, hey?"—and biting his nails even. So his brother left him to it.

With the Day of Judgement come, or so it appeared to Silas, it was a comfort for him to feel the darkness, wind and rain now rushing up to aid him, and the camouflaging presence of the trees. Silas gained the crest of the ridge and accelerated as he began to descend the further side. The thought flashed upon him: 'I am gonna make it!' Only then there was a terrible loud bang in the rear. He turned to see what it was, took too long—and rode into a tree.

Silas lay on the ground and studied the branch that had

fetched him off. His seeming allies were against him too.
He got to his feet, swaying, and gazed about with a baffled
air. His horse was gone, there was the sound of other
horsemen on the ridge, and his knee hurt. Silas's thoughts
were: (1) 'I have had it!' and, because that he was a
persevering stubborn man, (2) 'Maybe I will climb up this
tree.' Which he then did.

It is an ironical circumstance that the noise Silas had
heard and which was the ruination of him, came from
Jake. In haste to follow his brother, Jake had dislodged the
shotgun from his laded horse before yet he was in the
saddle. The gun went off, so did the horse—bolted; so too,
after some consideration of his plight, did Jake. The horse
fled in the direction of the cabin, associated in its mind,
perhaps, with memories of an earlier feed. (The other
theory is, it was just pointing that way.) And Jake went
running after.

Now the rescuers were arrived and the scene played out
beside the track was of a more joyful kind. Mrs Gains was
rushed at and hugged by Amos,

"Mama, Mama!"
untied by the old-timers,

"Howdy, ma'am!"

"Which way'd them varmints go?"
rushed at and hugged again by Miss Alice and a couple of
the Gals,

"Oh, my-o-my!"

"Oh, goodness!"

"Mrs Gains!"
and saluted, each in his own fashion, by Chief Afraid-of-
His-Mother and Captain Wilkie.

Well, that brave woman was not a little overwhelmed by these attentions. The truth is, she wept and clutched the now ever-snoozing baby to her, and hugged Amos the more. He wept, too, which was a puzzle to *him* on account of he could find no sadness in the occasion. (Amos was not yet of an age to appreciate the full versatility of tears in human life. There you are; eights do not have it all their own way.)

The concourse of people grew. There was a passing traffic of Indians and troopers scouting the Slocums' trail. The captain and the chief were shouting orders. Horses neighed and skidded on the slippery bank. The ground was churning up.

Ike arrived with a lamp from the ambulance and shook hands with Mrs Gains. The remaining Gals brought a slicker for her; the rain was coming heavier. Miss Alice held her parasol above the baby's head.

The mountain man was in there, too, lifting his flexible felt hat and expressing satisfaction at the happy outcome. Already, he had a good appreciation of what had taken place. But, of course, from talking French, his meaning was obscured. Until, that is, the chief spoke up, making use of his linguistical skill.

He said, "Mountain man, those words are a credit to you, and to your ancestors besides." And he said, "I would be much and permanently honoured to pass them on." Which, by a most elegant translation, he proceeded to do.

Mrs Gains, still somewhat overcome, gave thanks to everybody. In time, she would be curious to learn where Amos had discovered them all. For the present, the prior feelings of relief and thanksgiving held sway within her.

Mrs Gains said, "Your papa is not here, Amos?"

"No, Mama," Amos said. "I could not catch him up. He was sighted, though!"

"That is a fact," said the chief; and to himself added, "We could not catch him up either."

By now H. E. Burl had joined the crowd. He said, "I seen y'husband, Mrs Gains. He was thrivin'!"

"So he was," the first old-timer said. "We seen him, too!"

"Yeah," the second said. "Seen him—seen his pa, come to that ... once upon a time."

Mrs Gains put on the slicker, Miss Kitty holding the baby while she did it. Ike raised his lamp on high. Thereafter, H. E. Burl, from observing more closely the baby's snoozing form, the coolness and repose in its little face, the jaunty angle of the thumb in its little mouth, declared, "Yes sir, that baby is the genuine article—a true Gains!"

11

POTTER'S WOOD

TWENTY minutes later the baby was awake, sitting up snug in a set of dry clothes and attending earnestly to the spoonfuls of mush it was receiving from Miss Loretta. It had received spoonfuls beforehand from Miss Alice and Miss June. They were taking it in turns.

The action had transferred to the Gainses' cabin. A fire blazed and the ill-effects of siege and pillage were rapidly disappearing. Already the Slocums' horses had been caught, though not the Slocums, and much of the stolen property restored to its rightful place. However, the shotgun was still out in the rain, unnoticed, and a frying pan had been run over by the ambulance.

Mrs Gains and Amos supervised and lent a hand with the tidying up of the cabin. The mountain man and the chief were both prominent in this work. H. E. Burl made every effort to re-position the club chair, and then slumped down in it. The pungency of powder and hot metal lingered yet and stung in people's noses.

As the work proceeded, Amos and his ma swopped accounts of their adventures and mishaps during the day.

Amos spoke mostly of being chased by Indians. "I just kept my head down and rode, Mama."

"You did well, Amos." (Mrs Gains had heard about Jules Ridge by this time, from parties on *both* sides.)

"We would've got away, Mr Burl said, if the stage had not crashed. We would've been in Benson's Bend in no time!"

"Yes," said Mrs Gains, "I can believe it—Amos, put this bread-board on the table."

Amos did so. "Oh, but you should've seen the stage, Mama; it was covered with arrows! And when it crashed two wheels come off—"

"*Came* off," said Mrs Gains.

"—and one of them kept rolling by itself, right up the road! Then we had to make this barricade with the luggage, and then the Indians arrived and one of them had his feet turned in—like this!"

At this point Amos recalled the shell-beads the chief had given him. He showed them to his ma. The Barnes boot pistol, however, which he had tucked away in his belt, not boot, Amos failed to mention. He knew his ma would want to put it up for safe-keeping. As you can imagine, Amos much preferred the safe-keeping of it himself.

Mrs Gains, in her cool fashion, spoke of the siege. "The worst fear I had was that I might actually shoot somebody! Amos, put this book in the bookcase."

Amos did so.

"And I was thinking they would come down the chimney—here's another, Amos—and they came up through the floor!"

Amos said, "Our cabin is like a fort, Mr Burl says." And he said, "Can I take a look in the tunnel, Mama?"

Mrs Gains replaced the near-empty bag of buckshot on its shelf and gazed thoughtfully about for the shotgun. "Tomorrow, Amos—we'll both look."

(I should add that Amos and his ma, though eager for the return of Sheriff Gains, were not over-worried by his continued absence. His posses often did last several days. On one occasion he had rode clean out of the state.)

Besides feeding the baby, Miss Alice and the Gals were making large quantities of coffee. The coffee, mugs and pans were army issue. Of course civilians, Indians, too, were among those waiting in line.

It must be said, this drink, though hot, had little else to recommend it. The ladies were civilized, cosmopolitan even, but domesticated not in the least. Still, the service was good; more than one fellow came back a second and a third time only for the smile that attended the filling-up of his mug. An amount of 'army hard bread' was on offer also, but for this there were few takers.

Outside, beyond the vegetable garden, a number of troopers—volunteers and enthusiasts—were pitching a tent. It was a Sibley tent and big enough for twenty men. The troopers were getting lost in it and laughing mightily from the struggles they were having. In the main, the army had preferred to establish itself in the barn. Here an iron tent-stove had been set up and was glowing already in the doorway. The cook and his helpers were preparing a stew.

Elsewhere the search for the Slocum Boys continued. (It was known they could not have gone far, from the discovery of their horses.) Riders crossed and re-crossed over the dark land. Lamps flickered among the trees. Voices hailed one another above the buffeting of wind and rain. The Indians kept in touch by screeching like an owl and so forth. The Slocums were not found. Now and then the searchers went to some pains in capturing themselves; in error, you understand. The second old-timer, for instance, from looking so disreputable in his ruined hat and coat, got grabbed by a trooper. It was the trooper suffered most in the exchange.

Silas Slocum remained sat in his tree like a big wet bird. From the branch above, an actual big wet bird was watching him with a baleful eye; peeved by the intrusion, maybe. I guess creatures generally in Potter's Wood that night had cause for complaint. From time to time a rider would pass near or even below, a circumstance which, in his usual state of vigour, no Slocum Boy could fail to have took advantage of. But Silas now was wet and stiff and cold, and dazed yet from his fall, and downright apathetic. He had got into that tree with the last of his grit. For the present, he was stuck there.

Jake Slocum was in some ways better off. At least his hide-out was dry, cosy even. He had candles burning in there. You see, Jake was back in the tunnel again, about halfway along. He had arrived there like this. You will recall his running off after that horse. Well, he did not catch the horse. Fact is, in his panic and the gloom he overtook it. Then, with pursuers after him and scant choice in the matter, and a liking for such places anyway, he re-entered the tunnel. The disadvantage of Jake's position was that he could not think how to get out.

Furthermore, a whiff of coffee from somewhere was beginning to tantalize his nose.

Meanwhile, Sheriff Gains was coming home. By one means or another, he had brought the posse to Benson's Bend, from whence, with the light fading and the weather about to break, it had dispersed. The business with the Indians had not perturbed the men unduly. From the Indians seeing so little of the posse, it followed that the posse saw just as little of them. They hardly knew the mischief they had escaped from. A number even had agreed to meet next day for a continuation of the search. Sheriff Gains, of course, would not give up.

Well, every one of the men was pretty much whacked out, as you would expect, and looking forward to the peace and probable affections of his own abode. Only storekeeper Morris Hacker did not get it, I believe; the peace, that is. His wife was waiting for him with a blanket with a burn-hole in it.

"The twins done that," Mrs Hacker said, "on some alleged picnic; and I am plumb sick o' them boys, and how is it, Mr Hacker, you go swannin' off all round the county seekin' for criminals when there is two of 'em growing up right here in y'own house?"

Mr Hacker raised the blanket and stared disconsolately through the hole. "I will see about it," he said.

Upstairs the twins were listening hard. The thought came to one of them, 'I bet that blanket'd make a neat poncho!'

And the other said, "D'you figure the Indians have this kind of trouble when *they're* signallin'?"

So I think you will have got it now: it was the *Hacker Boys* who had supplied that 'Indian' smoke, which Ike had fled from or, for that matter, which the cavalry had turned back to investigate. 'Some boys up there fooling around', you see—just like the chief surmised.

Sheriff Gains was riding with Deputy Smout. They were neighbours; it was his field of corn the posse had set off through. Deputy Smout, from being a bachelor, was invited to the Gainses' place to eat. The wind and rain made conversation difficult. Each man tucked in his chin and became occupied with his own thoughts.

Deputy Smout thought about a birthday present for Sheriff Gains. He had a couple of things in mind but could not decide between them. One was a compass. He feared a spirit of mockery might be read into such a gift, which was not his intention. Maybe he would have a private word with Mrs Gains. He thought about the condition of his own head. It was substantially bandaged up under his hat and, following a period of quiescence, was beginning to throb. Then he compared himself unfavourably with Sheriff Gains. Deputy Smout admired Sheriff Gains for his courage, his determination and, above all, his uncluttered response to the problems of life. With him it was not, 'Well, on the one hand, then on the other'. He did not fret to see a situation from all sides. He was not always waiting around. No sir, he set off and the result was, he *got* somewhere. Deputy Smout was an ambivalent man, you see. He could not even make up his mind to sit on the fence.

Sheriff Gains, as befits a married man, was thinking of his family. His affection for Mrs Gains seemed only to increase with the passage of time. He was ever glad to be returning to her. The baby was a fascination to him. To see so small a thing with so much character; it had been the same with Amos. (It would be the same with subsequent babies, too. The Gains family had not come to a halt, by no means.) Amos, for his part, was just the kind of steadfast son that he had hoped for. In the morning, maybe, he would have Amos read to him a page from Parson Weems's *Life of Washington*.

But Sheriff Gains was giving thought to more professional considerations, too. There was the situation of the horses in Hanksville, that needed to be sorted out. And what was Sheriff Moody up to, he wondered. Had he given up yet? And Sheriff de Grasse, whose trail he had mislaid. And the Slocum Boys, of course; where were they?

So Sheriff Gains led Deputy Smout home. They were not travelling by the most direct route—the rain on Sheriff Gains's glasses had reduced his field of vision even more—but they were getting there. By and by, they began to climb the wooded slope of a familiar ridge. It was not far now. The anticipation of domestic bliss—hot food, dry clothes, a jug of beer before the fire—was working its effect on the two men. Rain gathered and fell in great drips from the trees, the wind blew noisily in the branches while yet the sheriff and his deputy passed on obliviously below.

After a time Deputy Smout said, or rather hollered so as to be heard, "Osgood, is that a light I can see?" and pointed up ahead, "Hey, Osgood—what d'you think?"

Sheriff Gains reined in his horse, took off his glasses, gave them a wipe, put them back and said, "I cannot see a thing."

Nor for that matter could Deputy Smout, now. For one circumstance, the light—if it was a light—had disappeared. For another, a big heavy man had just fell on him out of a tree.

'Fell' was the word. Later, at Silas's trial, the defence were to insist on it; nor were the prosecution disposed to argue. Silas did fall; from the condition he was in, it was the most he could have managed. Picture the scene. There was Silas perched in his tree and sunk into a frozen trance; aside from all else, he had not slept in two days. Through his mind there passed a dishonestly remembered sequence of exploits from his criminal career: a train job here, a bank job there; a bit of rustling one long green summer in Selina County; a fried catfish lifted from the general store in Brown Willow. He had been but six years old then. That fish was bigger'n him.

Then, a-seeping into his ear like the rain through his hat, came voices. Silas stirred on his branch. There was a name here he could identify—'Osgood'. What was the significance of that? He stirred some more; endeavoured to grasp the fugitive notion in his brain, failed to grasp the tree itself, and departed from it.

Thus it was that Deputy Smout took a fresh knock on his head and was besides dumped off his horse and into the mud. In an instant, and heedless of his own accumulated wounds, Sheriff Gains leapt to his aid. The three men began thrashing about on the ground, the law officers calling to each other. You see, Deputy Smout retained yet his wits and his spirit, too. It was a glancing blow he had took.

"I am with you, George!"

"You got him, Osgood? I cannot tell if I have his leg or yourn!"

Silas did not speak. The truth is, he did not struggle overmuch either. He was confused. He did not know what was happening *before* he had fell. However, Sheriff Gains and Deputy Smout were not to know this. From the righteous vigour of their efforts, they had Silas in pretty constant motion. In the darkness there was the illusion of a desperate foe; while in the mud, to get a grip on anything at all, it was like catching an oiled pig.

At the finish it was done. The unresisting outlaw was subdued and the law officers, after a necessary spell of gasping for breath, set to considering what they had caught.

12

THE CABIN

WHEN Sheriff Gains and Deputy Smout arrived at the cabin with Silas Slocum, they still were not sure it was him. A couple of troopers, Independence Ike and an Indian had joined them on the way in. They threw metaphorical light on the situation with their account of recent events, and real light, too, in the form of Ike's lamp. (Ike had been taking part in the search, another instance of the continuing shift in his character.) It was realized, therefore, that likely one of the Slocums had been took—but which one? As brothers, they possessed considerable physical similarity. Besides, this man was all dirtied-up. He had so much mud on him, even his shape was camouflaged. Efforts to wipe it off seemed only to reveal more layers underneath. You will recall, Silas was all dirtied-up from his previous fall, and the tunnelling, too. Also, parts of him never were clean.

Recognition of the law officers was not straightforward either. Deputy Smout had lost his hat and looked to be wearing a brown turban. Sheriff Gains's sling, which could have identified him to the Indians, had now the appearance of a piece of rope, and was not in use. His badge was barely visible. He had put his muddied-up glasses away.

Mrs Gains knew him, though; so did Amos.

"Osgood!"

"Papa, Papa!"

Whereupon the three did embrace and kiss in one close triangle of family affection.

Amos said, "I was looking out for you, Papa!"

"So I hear, Amos," his pa said.

They spread the sheriff's rain and mud to and fro between them with never a care.

Amos said, "I was in the hills with Mr H. E. Burl—we ate a turkey! I was in a *saloon*!"

Mrs Gains scooped up the baby, "Come on, Emily, you should have a cuddle, too," and drew her into the proceedings.

Amos said, "Mr Burl says, do not misuse a mule he will remember you for it."

"That's good advice, Amos," his pa said.

Sheriff Gains kissed the baby, and was on target. His sense of relief was then all bodied forth in one intensifying hug. He raised his family off the ground for a while.

Amos protested, "Help, I am being crushed!"

"A grizzly has got us!" Mrs Gains declared.

The baby burped.

The crowd in the cabin looked on with a sympathetic eye. Chief Afraid-of-His-Mother took a particular interest. From the behaviour of Mrs Gains, he deduced that here was Sheriff Gains come back. Evidently he had caught his man. Chief Afraid-of-His-Mother felt the sensation of respect growing in his heart for Sheriff Gains. (Forget not that there had been upwards of a hundred Indians out there looking for him.)

Earlier the chief had been occupied with the rainfall they were having. He pondered the likelihood of his mother's involvement in it. Now a wider sense of mystery possessed his thoughts. He had a vision of the countless tracks men leave across the land. Even before a man could walk, while yet he was carried on his mother's back, he had begun to trace his mark. The magical ride of Sheriff Gains was but a part of the enigma of his whole life's passage, that was itself one little thread in the vast weave of human life upon this earth. The chief took a sip of his coffee. He had resolved the mystery—merged it, you might say, in a larger—and was content.

Silas Slocum stood like a clayman in the centre of the room. Sheriff Gains cleaned off his glasses and regarded him. He—the sheriff, that is—was in a rare state of indecision. It was his public duty to uphold the law. It was his private wish to knock Silas down a few times. He had knocked Silas down a few times in Potter's Wood. But then he did not know how well the man deserved it. Nor did Silas know who was hitting him, or why.

"A man should know why he is being hit, George," the sheriff said.

"I guess so," said Deputy Smout. He was seated at the table having his head re-bandaged by Miss Loretta. "And who he is hittin'—hey, Osgood?"

Deputy Smout intended no irony by this remark, but was referring to the prisoner's identity—still uncertain.

Amos had positioned himself slightly behind his pa. He was very interested to see an outlaw close to. Considering the nature of his pa's trade, he had seldom done so.

Amos said, "Would you say I was old enough to have a gun, Papa?" (Amos knew he must reveal the Barnes boot pistol eventually, and was preparing the ground.)

Sheriff Gains's indecision vanished. "A gun—yes; bullets—no."

Amos weighed this up for a minute. It was not the best answer he could have had; it did not confirm the old-timers' opinions, for instance, but it would do to be going on with. He returned to studying Silas Slocum.

Amos looked for scars or other marks of villainy, but with all that dirt was disappointed. He recalled the talk which Mr W. 'Bigfoot' Wallace had given at the school. It was more about outlaws than anything else. Mr Wallace said an outlaw had a singular look in his eye that the true law officer ever could detect. Amos watched this outlaw's eye for a time, in hopes of seeing what it was.

Word of Silas's capture was making its way among the hardy fellows yet persisting with the search, which did include the old-timers. When they heard, they came to the cabin and gave some scrutiny to Silas. He was beginning to revive and gave them some scrutiny back.

"Which one we got here, Silas or Jake?"

"Who brung him in?"

The tale was told.

"Ah well, I knowed his pa, y'know—and yourn."

The old-timers were offered coffee by Miss June, which they refused, and a nip of 'Riffler's' rum by Sheriff Gains, which they did not. The sheriff had the baby in the crook of one arm as he poured with the other.

The first old-timer said, "Whoa there!", but only when his glass was full. He peered at the baby. A drip of rain ran off his hat and baptized its little head. "Jest look at that! T'figure we was ever one of them."

His cousin peered, too. He inhaled the baby's sweet clean smell. He marvelled at the miniature perfection of its fingernails. "Let's see here; when this infant is as old as me—I'm as old as a rock—it'll be ..."

"His ma were a midwife, y'know," the first old-timer said.

"It'll be ... 1956!"

Now Mrs Gains stepped forward. She wished to offer more extended thanks to the old-timers for what they had done. But the old-timers could see no call for it, and were embarrassed. They ducked their heads, scratched their rough chins and left pretty soon after. Besides, they were keen to continue the search. They dearly aspired to catch an outlaw for themselves; for Sheriff de Grasse, too, of course.

Silas Slocum kept on with his revival. In the heat of the room he was observed bit by bit to be baking out. Cracks appeared in the deposits on his boots and clothes. Flakes of dried mud fell off his head and gathered about him on the floor. (Amos, with his steady gaze, witnessed a scar unveiled.) As he recovered, Silas obtained a better appreciation of the fix he was in. This brought him to an ill humour and the utterance of vile epithets at a fearful rate, regardless of the ladies and Amos—and the baby—who were present. He became completely anxious that everyone should go to the devil.

At this point, Silas was directed to quit his noise by a number of the men. "We will duck y'in the trough, if'n y'don't!" So he did; but shortly after started up again. This time he took a more ingratiating line, though with what end in view it is hard to imagine. They were not going to let him go!

"There has been irregularities in my conduct, I will allow." Silas could speak nicely when he had a mind to. "Yet I never meant no harm. I thought we could get him—that's Sheriff Gains, there—get him, and dust him up some, for what he done to us. But it was not to be. There y'are, a man's fondest hopes is oft-times broke with trouble." Silas shuffled his feet. An amount of mud and small twigs clattered to the floor. "Anyways, it was all Jake's idea!"

So then they *knew* it was Silas.

Meanwhile, Jake had been working his way up the tunnel. From being lonesome, he was humming a tune and talking to himself. In the beginning he had had a rational thought or two concerning his situation, e.g. lying up (down) where he was till things got quiet. He could hear and *feel* the steady traffic in the yard above his head.

Slowly, however, he began to lose the little good sense and sound judgement he possessed. Fantasies of an ever wilder nature came into his brain. He even played with the notion of digging a fresh tunnel to somewhere else!

Well, first it was the coffee smell luring him on, then the companionable buzz of voices he could hear. Soon the sounds of people having a happy time—the laughing, the clinking of mugs—became too much for Jake. He felt a deep and melancholy pity for himself, and said so: "I am stuck here for life. I am *worser* off than ever I was!"

It is possible now that Jake would have had one

more rational thought and give himself up—he was actually in the cellar—had not a burst of adroit and, what is more important, *familiar* swearing come suddenly down to him from the room above.

Jake's spirits rose. "That is m'brother!"

You will appreciate, he was not uplifted to find Silas had been took, only that he was near. Moreover, in that fast and tricky way which even the slowest brains do things, he had already conceived the idea of a stupendous rescue, and pictured to himself at least two versions of the wondrous and dramatic scene.

It had always been one of the pleasures in Jake's life to have Silas read to him from the papers. He enjoyed to hear the exploits of notable men: 'Dutch' Henry, George W. Flatt, lawman or desperado, it did not signify. He admired the headlines particularly, and could recite whole columns word perfect:

PURSUING THE ROBBERS
SHERIFF MASTERSON HEARD FROM
WITHIN TWO HOURS RIDE OF THE
BRIGANDS
A PROBABLE DEADLY ENCOUNTER

Above all, it was his delight to be holed-up in a snug den with the loot, a sandwich and a jug of rye, and be in bed, and have his own exploits read to him. Funny thing was, they mostly sounded better in the papers. Silas's plans just seemed to come out niftier in black and white. He, Jake, said smarter things when they was reported than ever he could recollect doing at the time.

Thus Jake could see it all before him:

SLOCUMS RETRIEVE THEIR FORTUNES
WITH A BOLD DISPLAY
FIFTY PISTOLS PRESSED TO HIS HEAD
COME AWAY UNSCATHED AND HIS
BROTHER WITH HIM

This was a tonic for Jake. He clutched his gun—THE PERSUASIVE POWER OF A '44—and listened beneath the cellar trap. He hoped to gauge the disposition of forces ranged against him. Once more it illustrates the speed of human thought, when I record

that what Jake was hearing was yet the back-end of Silas's tirade.

So there you have it, and pretty much for the last time. One roomful of honest citizens, their duty done, enjoying the consciousness of troubles come to a halt. One ruffian in the cellar all poised to set them going again.

About the room, as Silas first ranted and subsequently wheedled on, some were listening, some were not.

H. E. Burl continued to take his ease in the club chair. He watched the moths blundering round the lamp. He nibbled on a piece of 'hard tack'. "'In the sweat of thy brow shalt thou eat bread'," he said to himself; "or try to." He heard talk of stew from the troopers in the coffee line. He went forth to investigate.

Captain Wilkie was engaged with Miss Alice in an exchange of views on the subject of American literature. Had she by chance read Mr Herman Melville's latest book? It was assuredly a wonderful and seriously intentioned work. She had not. Was she perhaps familiar with the works of Mrs Louisa Orne Blewett? She was not. Or Doctor Oliver Wendell Holmes? No.

The fact is, Miss Alice did not have too much time for literature. She would own that Beadle's *Dime Book of Fun* was a very fine work, otherwise her opinions were limited. Anyway, she did not suppose they were really talking about literature. She supposed Captain Wilkie was trying to get acquainted. In the long run, I will say, Captain Wilkie was to fail in this enterprise. Maybe, if he had not kept calling her Miss 'Frimm', things would have been different.

The mountain man and Miss Sadie were preoccupied with language. It had become understood between them that their communications problem would be solved from him learning English, not her French. Wherefore he was pointing at objects in the room and she was naming them.

"*Qu'est ce que c'est?*" (Meaning, "What's that?")

"A tin of shoe blacking: shoe black-ing."

"Shoo bla-keen. *Et ça?*" ("And that?")

"A medicine chest: me-di-cine chest."

They were using mime and drawing pictures with Amos's retrieved pencil. There was good will on both sides. Progress was being made.

Deputy Smout was telling Amos the tale of his bandaged head. "I foolishly got in your papa's way when we was changin' horses."

"Was it a horse-kick then, Mr Smout?" Amos said.

"It was your papa's elbow, Amos." Deputy Smout raised a hand to his clean bandages and winced. "He is a man of action, y'know."

Now, besides listening to the deputy, Amos was doing two other things: (1) entertaining the baby with an eagle's feather; (2) I regret to say, giving no small moiety of attention to Silas's virtuoso cussing. 'The Hacker Boys know a few words,' Amos thought, 'but nothing like this.'

Deputy Smout, for his part, had one eye on the cellar trap. He could not make up his mind whether he had lately seen it move.

Meanwhile, under the floor there was Jake a-crouching. Thin bars of light shone through the cracks between the boards. The last candle had guttered away. A fine dust descended and covered his shoulders and hat. Temporarily, Jake forgot the events of the day. He had the feeling he had been here before. It seemed to him he almost knew the future, too; only he could not say what it was.

Jake was ready. "I'm gonna go now!" he said. "I'm gonna count three and go. One ... Two ... I'm gonna have a peep first, then go! Now I'm gonna go. I'm gonna count three." But thereafter, when truly he was going to go, or might well have done, he overheard those words of Silas's: "It was all Jake's idea!"

Jake was stunned. The disloyalty of the remark, the injustice of it, the knowledge that he would never in similar circumstances have thought of saying the same thing about Silas—yet in that case it would have been the truth—came close to deranging his already hard-pressed mental apparatus. Thus, whether he heard what else Silas was saying—which was in general to blacken his, Jake's, character and expose him as the kind of mean skunk what did bad things hisself and egged-on close members of his family to follow suit—is not known. Though he picked up a word, as you will see. What is known, is that Jake came flying up out of the cellar like a rocket or the devil in some religious play, leapt on Silas and began to beat the day-lights out of him. It was a change of plan, you will observe.

Well, this was like beating a carpet. The clouds of dust came billowing out. There was the thump of pummellings delivered, the groan of pummellings received, to say nothing of Jake hollering the while: "All that's a pack o' lies, Silas, I never had no ideas in m'life, and who are you to call a other man a skunk what are y'self the president and king o' skunks?" And much else. (I should point out, Jake had not his gun with him; he would not *shoot* Silas, anyway; but it was back there in the cellar.)

The people in the room were dumbfounded by this event. It was a thunderclap for them. It was a thunderclap for Silas. However, soon a lively stampede did commence. Efforts were made to interfere with what already many suspicioned to be the *fraternal* fisticuffs they were witness to. Miss Loretta, for one, had thoughts of using the furni-ture to put an end to the scrape. It was well for the safety of the chair and Jake's head that the ambulance sergeant laid a restraining hand on her.

Then somebody said, "Hold on there, they'm doin' all right!"

And another, "That's the ticket—let 'em be!"

In double-quick time a circle formed up around the milling pugilists. Amos was there, muscling in between Ike and Captain Wilkie.

Captain Wilkie said, "I understand we have got Slocker versus Slocker here."

Ike said, "Slocum—yeah, though I cannot say f'sure. They always wore masks in my presence."

And the captain said, "Sheriffs will be out of a job, if this keeps up!"

Comments arose now concerning the finer points of the

action. Small bets were placed upon the outcome. Amos kept his eyes fixed on the dusty figures trading blows. The thought in *his* mind was, 'Who'll cry uncle?'

The outcome in normal circumstances would have been a win for Silas. He was the toughest, though not the meanest, as I have said. Meanness and toughness are two different things. But Silas was in a poor way. He had beforehand been in a fight. Thereto the elements of dash and surprise, plus what little righteousness there was around, were all working for Jake. So Silas was getting the worst of it. Odds of 4-9 were quoted in his behalf.

Sheriff Gains prepared to intervene. "My sense of duty is getting the better of me, George."

"I can appreciate that, Osgood."

"I cannot stand by and allow the law to be so disregarded in my own house!"

"No, y'surely can't."

"All the same, the rough justice in the situation does not escape me."

"Nor me, Osgood; I can see it!"

But before the sheriff or his deputy could make a move—while, in truth, they were still debating it—the mountain man stepped in and saved them the trouble. He seized Jake in one mighty hand by the back of his coat, Silas in the other, and held them out.

Jake, quite crazed now, was yet swinging his fists in a snappy way at the invisible air, and spinning somewhat, like an apple on a string. Silas was as near used-up as a man can be. He only hung there.

The mountain man smiled at Miss Sadie and raised Silas up. "*Qu'est ce que c'est?*"

Miss Sadie said, "A outlaw: a out-law!"

"*Et ça?*" The mountain man raised Jake up.

"Another outlaw!"

The mountain man smote the Slocum Boys against each other once or twice, which had the effect of slowing Jake down. Then, because that he never was a vengeful fellow, he arranged them back-to-back on the floor. Whence they were content to remain.

13

ALL OVER

NOW was there much jubilation in the Gainses' cabin. Soon it was Munn's 'Special Rye' all round—army issue—and root beer for Amos. Mugs were raised and noble sentiments expressed in the form of many toasts.

H. E. Burl, with a mess-can of stew now in his possession, set it aside and stood on a chair. "Ladies and gents, I'm a minister of the Lord and teetotal in accordance with His Word. But I shall drink tonight!"

A trooper cheered.

"I shall drink t'the honour of this boy, Amos Gains. His was a ride like Paul Revere's!"

They all drank to that. Some ate to it too; the stew-pot in the barn was gaining custom. Amos had a plateful, which Mr Burl had brought back with his own. He said, "I have read about Paul Revere in my McGuffey reader."

H. E. Burl continued. "I shall drink to his ma, than whom there is none braver. His er, sister there, the genuinest little article y'ever seen. And his pa, Sheriff Gains, positively a lawman like no other!"

They all drank to that. More cheering and applause took place, plus a burst of shield-banging from the three or four Indians present. Thereafter Mr Burl wobbled briefly on his chair and got down.

Other toasts followed. 'H. E. Burl' was proposed by Sheriff Gains, and 'The U.S. Cavalry' by Chief Afraid-of-His-Mother. Independence Ike drank a couple of toasts to himself, which he said he deserved. He was grown melancholy from recalling the condition of the stage, and his disorganized schedule. Captain Wilkie returned the chief's compliment and also gave Miss Alice a quiet toast on her own. 'To the brightest ornament . . .', that kind of thing. He was still calling her Miss Frimm, though.

It was at this time somebody spotted the Slocums were not drinking.

"What about them? Don't they git any?"

Another said, "Yeah, where's the fairness in that? Hadn't 'a' been for them, wouldn't be no celebrations needed!"

Well, I guess there is a speck of truth in that. 'The dark is necessary to the light', as they say. Every mortal thing has its appointed work; even a Slocum.

So the Slocum Boys received their mugs and raised them to the next toast: 'A deputy's pluck', and the one following: 'Down with outlaws'. Jake did show a certain dignity at first. "I won't drink with him (meaning Silas). I was there poised to save his very bacon, y'know. He is a snake." But he did all the same.

121

By and by, the last toast was drunk, or maybe they ran out of Munn's. The last ladlefuls of stew were served. The last bowls and plates scraped clean, licked clean and generally polished off.

Now of a sudden Amos was yawning and heavy-eyed. At the behest of his ma, he went to bed. On the stairs the thought in his mind was, 'I never looked at the chickens!' But those fowl were safe enough. They had not ended up in the stew, if you were thinking so.

Amos set his candle down beside the bed and crossed to the window. His boots crunched on broken glass from a couple of its panes. Outside the rain had ceased. The mass of cloud was breaking up and scudding over the sky. Amos blinked and stared into the dark yard. He wondered about the tunnel and who would get to fill it up; and the old-timers still, it seemed, out searching; and the broken glass in the windows and the portrait of President Grant.

That tunnel and broken glass were evidence, Amos thought: the proof that anything had ever happened at all. For already a haze was forming over the events of the day; already they were not so *real* as they had been. Amos felt the shell-beads in his pocket—there was a proof; and the gun in his belt—there was another! He had a cavalry cap badge, too—crossed sabres in stamped brass—which a trooper had given him.

Amos yawned. He drew the curtains, put the Barnes boot pistol under his pillow and got ready for bed.

In the room below, the ambulance sergeant sat down at the piano and struck a chord. The cry arose, "Give us, 'Natchez-under-the-Hill'!" "Give us, 'Frog Mountain'!" Which he did.

Singing began. Miss Kitty and Miss June did not take part on account of they had fell asleep; but Miss Loretta did. She was the enthusiast of all time, Miss Loretta. When it was the croquet craze, she played croquet like a fiend. In later years, when the bicycle craze came along, she rode a bicycle like a fiend. Now, with a few of the more tuneful troopers, Miss Loretta led the way through sundry choruses of 'Northern Belle', 'Goodbye Old Paint', 'Tuck Me in My Little Bed' and 'The Battle Hymn of the Republic'. The ambulance sergeant passed complimentary remarks regarding the piano. Sheriff and Mrs Gains performed a duet: 'Gone Where the Woodbine Twineth'. They ever enjoyed a musical turn. Deputy Smout whistled along. H. E. Burl sang a hymn.

Then at the finish even Miss Loretta's abundant energy ran out. She dozed off in the club chair; H. E. Burl was favouring the sofa at this time. The proceedings came gradually to a halt.

By midnight most were sleeping. The cabin and barn were crowded with rolls and humps of army blankets. They stirred with the slow rhythm of sleep. (The Sibley tent had been given up on.) In the ambulance the Slocums were handcuffed and under guard. It hardly signified. They were too worn out and befuddled to care. You could not have paid them to escape that night. You could not have chased them off.

On Jules Ridge a party of homeward-wending Indians had stopped to light a fire and were snoozing beside it. In Hanksville, with an undrunk mug of cocoa at his elbow, Sheriff de Grasse was asleep in his office. He had come back with the posse. They too were sleeping—the piano-player, tailor and all. Over in Tuscalero County, in the peace and comfort of that neat house of his, Sheriff Chas. H. Moody was a-sleeping likewise. In his case he had been doing so for no little time.

Some were not sleeping. In Hanksville across the street from Sheriff de Grasse, a light shone in the Bella Union Hotel. The prospectors, having had their sleep out, were sitting up in bed and playing cards. Down the street at the livery stable, H. E. Burl's mules were wakeful and kicking up a fuss: for a bit of fresh feed, certainly, and—if you will believe such things of dumb animals—a bit of Mr Burl's companionship to go with it.

Beyond the river and under the once-more cloudless sky, other parties of Indians were trotting on towards the reservation. They observed the friendly constellations in the large chaos of heaven. They whooped, once in a while, the younger ones, from a rousing recollection of the day's events.

One Indian had taken the opportunity to roam. He rode by the Hacker place and the restless boys there—they had cause from Mr Hacker for being in this state—saw him go. They pressed their faces to the glass and marvelled how they had conjured him up.

In the Gainses' corral a couple of troopers were stood watch over the army's gear and precious horses. In the yard the old-timers were stood watch over the ambulance. The old-timers were cooking a pan of beans and drinking beer. Despite previous disappointments and some of the fun they had missed, the old fellows were glowing now from inner satisfaction. They were enrolled as deputies by Sheriff Gains! When the trial came they would assuredly give evidence. All Hanksville would sit up when they got the news.

Amos was awake, too, but only just. He had been disturbed in his sleep by a noise. He lay with his eyes open but could not think where he was. Some business about the Yellow Day of 1810 was in his mind ... a snake sunning itself on a rock . . . a puff of smoke. 'I have got a bullet-hole in the end of my bed,' he recalled. His eyes were shut again. A smell of beans came to his nose—and turkey! Murmurous voices were below the window; this which had woke him up. He was asleep.

Outside on the porch three voices in two languages rose up into the night. It was Miss Sadie and the mountain man intent upon their life's advancement. You see, such linguistical progress as they had made, had not kept pace with the acceleration of their hearts' affections, or indeed ever got close to it. Now they were sat with the chief beside them, as they had been for a time and would be for a time yet, passing the phrases of their courtship back and forth with the aid of that obliging man. Chief Afraid-of-His-Mother felt no urgency to leave. The current of fond words flowed through him. It was a good end to the day.